THE WOMAN AT THE WINDOW

Marian Eldridge attracted critical acclaim with her first collection of stories, *Walking the Dog* (UQP 1984). Since then, she has had numerous stories published in anthologies and journals in Australia and overseas, including *Best Short Stories 1986* (Heinemann) and, more recently, *Canberra Tales* (Penguin 1988).

Marian Eldridge has travelled in Europe, the United States, South America, South Africa and remote parts of Australia. She is presently writing full-time in Canberra, where she is well known as a reviewer for the *Canberra Times*. *The Woman at the Window* is Marian Eldridge's second collection of stories.

THE WOMAN AT THE WINDOW

Marian Eldridge

University of Queensland Press

First published 1989 by University of Queensland Press,
Box 42, St Lucia, Queensland, Australia

Typeset by University of Queensland Press
Printed in Australia by The Book Printer, Melbourne

Distributed in the USA and Canada by
International Specialized Book Services, Inc.,
5602 N.E. Hassalo Street, Portland, Oregon 97213-3640

Creative writing program assisted by
the Literature Board of the Australia
Council, the Federal Government's arts
funding and advisory body

Cataloguing in Publication Data
National Library of Australia

Eldridge, Marian, 1936– .
   The woman at the window.

   I. Title.

A823'.3

ISBN 0 7022 2200 3

To my mother
GWEN STOCKFELD
always interested, always encouraging

CONTENTS

ACKNOWLEDGMENTS

These stories have previously appeared, with some differences, in the following publications: "Primavera" in *Southerly* 1 (1985); *Coast to Coast*, ed. Kerryn Goldsworthy (Angus & Robertson, Publishers, 1986); *Best Short Stories 1986*, ed. Giles Gordon and David Hughes (Heinemann: London, 1986); "Outside the Silver Dory" in *Quadrant* 1 (1984); "Pietà" in *Luna* 20 (1985); "A Sea Story" in *This Australia* 4, no. 3 (1985); "At the Signora's" in *The Australian Literary Magazine* April 6-7, 1985; Transgressions: Australian Writing Now, ed. Don Anderson (Penguin Books Australia Ltd, 1986); *The Australian Bedside Book*, ed. Geoffrey Dutton (Macmillan Australia, 1987); "Harvest" in *Southerly*, 1 (1986); "A Sense of Place" (as "Black and White: a prose miniature") in *Muse* 13 (December 1981-1982); "Pieces of Furniture" in *Muse* 57 (August 1986); "Students" in *The Australian Literary Magazine*, October 4-5, 1986; "Tourist" in *Kunapipi* vii, nos 2-3 (1985) (published simultaneously as *A Double Colonization: Colonial and Post-Colonial Women's Writing*, ed. Kirsten Holst Petersen and Anna Rutherford, [Dangaroo Press, 1986]); and in *Home and Away: Travel Stories*, ed. Rosemary Creswell (Penguin Books Australia Ltd, 1987); "Storm" in *Southerly* 4 (1987); "A Love Story" in *Kunapipi* viii, no 1, (1986); "What's the Time, Mr

Wolf?'' in *Southerly* 3 (1987); ''Capital Gains'' in *Canberra Tales*, Seven Writers (Penguin Books Australia Ltd, 1988).

In "Settle Down Country", the story about the night parrot is my own invention.

In "Capital Gains", the lines of verse quoted are from Tennyson's poems "The Lady of Shalott", "The Princess" and "Boadicea".

PRIMAVERA

Aunt Chrissie Jennaway has invited Alvie Skerritt down to Melbourne for the August school holidays. She's Alvie's aunt, Joan Skerritt's sister, the one who swapped country for city, and married money.

Alvie can't wait. She's fed up with this hoon town, fed up with her cranky, jangling family. What is there here that she wants to do? She knows every shop window by heart. She would like someone to talk to, maybe, but what is it she wants to say? *What?* she demands.

Her father, Ray Skerritt — he's the shop steward out at the paper mill, and he's always on about something, job sharing, industrial safety, Alvie's last maths test — he says You're off to a silly life, just don't get ideas Alvie.

Why are men always so bossy, why can't they just leave you alone?

Alvie shrugs: I can take care of myself. Joan Skerritt, her mouth full of pins because she is hemming Alvie's new skirt for Melbourne, jabs Ray Skerritt with a look: Chrissie is my sister, Ray, do you *mind?*

Scenting battle, the little kids sparkle.

Alvie looks at her family and sighs.

In what way silly, she wants to know. It's no big deal is it to want a bit of fun instead of the ever-present boiled cabbage stink of the paper mill, and a houseful of kids and trampled toys and homework and washing all over the place which as far as Alvie can see is about all that her mother has got from her father. A female's life is shithouse. So Cass Jawkins reckons. She's only in Alvie's year but she's got it all sussed out: look after number one. Yeah right, says Alvie, in that singsong surprised tone that everyone's using just now.

"Do stand still, Alv!" complains Joan Skerritt through the pins. "Do you want me to get this hem straight or don't you?"

Alvie can't wait to get on that train.

But if the mill town's a bore, it turns out life in Melbourne is no great riot either. Dragging after Aunt Chrissie first thing to admire a floppy new pansy or a bulb poking through a mush of leaf litter. Watching Aunt Chrissie bid for an old chair that Alvie thinks should go straight to the tip. Having cakes and coffee together in posh little shops where Alvie's appetite shrivels just thinking what her father would say about the prices. Then home to Uncle Rupert who's a prune, and that enormous squeaky-clean house where from the fancy three-piece mirror in her bedroom Alvie catches her triple image looking sideways at her homemade skirt.

What's more, because it's school holidays, any day now that wimpy kid Philip Jennaway will turn up. Philip Jennaway is Uncle Rupert's son by his first marriage. Alvie remembers Philip as one of those top-of-the-class kids too dumb not to show it. He is not due at the Jennaways' until two or three days after Alvie arrives because, Aunt Chrissie explains, his mother always makes some difficulty about his spending the entire vacation with his father. Aunt Chrissie grows quite fierce about this. "You'd think just this once — particularly when he hasn't any brothers or sisters of his own — but she always was a selfish woman." Suddenly she lowers her voice. "She refused him his conjugals, Alvie."

Alvie takes a moment to realise it's not Philip she means but Uncle Rupert, that stooped grey man who during dinner will clear his throat and hawk "And what did you do today, young woman?"

What did you do, young woman? Alvie's thoughts go skittering off to all the outings lately in the Gilberts' old panel van. Would Uncle Rupert swallow the story that the mattress Butch Gilbert has in the back is just a bit of showing-off to impress his mates? Despair like dirty bath water washes over Alvie. She's fed up with flogging the same old line, "Yes of course he behaves himself" to her parents, and to Butch Gilbert "No you can't — next time maybe — right now I've got you-know-what, it's just started, I've got, you know, *Charlie*." That's what girls have to say. He falls for it every time.

Changing out of her jeans into her skirt for dinner because that's the custom at Jennaways', Alvie tiptoes across to the three-piece mirror. Well, Alvie? The whole room is holding its breath. Alvie holds her breath too, squeezes up her eyes, tries hard for the sting of tears in her nose — a gaggle of girls crying together, but no tears come. So she studies her reflection, trying to make sense of it, trying to put together what she sees: three skinny girls with small, tense breasts, flat stomachs, hip bones sticking out like the wings on Uncle Rupert's leather chair. And inside, under the clothes, under the skin, the secret bones and veins and pulses, pumping blood, getting ready for Charlie, holding her together but all for what? She turns slowly, raising her arms, and thinks about a picture she has seen in some art book at school: three girls, arms lifted, absorbed in movement, oblivious of gawkers as wearing nothing but see-through nighties they dance barefoot in a garden. *Asking for it, got up like that* snicker the gawkers as one of the girls gets jumped by some yobbo . . . She thinks about her mother, kitchen images mostly, and that time she was pregnant with Lurlene, tight as a watermelon, you could see her navel when the wind blew her smock. In Grade Five Cass Jawkins wouldn't believe that babies didn't come out through your navel. You could laugh at Cass Jawkins then. But not now, Cass Jawkins makes out she knows everything now. And what after all is there to get so excited about, says Cass Jawkins. Just a guy slobbering on you and a bit of discomfort, a bit of blood.

Yeah, just a bit of blood, echoes Alvie Skerritt. A female's life is ruled by blood.

But what does Alvie Skerritt know about anything? She knows enough to scrape through most exams. She knows that the first Mrs Jennaway wouldn't give Uncle Rupert his conjugals and that this is a terrible thing, not natural Aunt Chrissie declares. She knows, from mooching around in the garden, the place where Philip Jennaway once built a treehouse, now abandoned like elastics or marbles. And where will any of *that* get Alvie?

Your age Alvie is the springtime of your life, her father tells her. Alvie reckons it's more like going into a maths test with only bits of the formulas inked on to her palm. They will all wake up to her one of these days — her parents, Butch Gilbert, knowing Cass Jawkins — and then what will she do?

Going downstairs for their pre-dinner sherry that makes Alvie secretly giddy, she finds that Philip has arrived. One glance at him and she ducks back upstairs to put on her special black lipstick. Oh golly, that Philip! My cousin in Melbourne's *gor*-geous, my cousin's a real hunk o' spunk, she practises telling Cass Jawkins. "Hel*lo* nice to see you again Alvie," he intones, and gives her a peck on the cheek.

He has a faint moustache now and he wears his hair longer, spunky, she tells Cass Jawkins. "White thanks Dad," he says in that supercool voice. Uncle Rupert pours him a glass of wine instead of sherry and he stands swirling his glass and perving over it. This so intrigues Alvie that she practises with her sherry, moving her glass under her nose as she drinks in Philip. He'd be as tall now as Butch Gilbert, not as lunky though. His wrists escape from his coat sleeves like flyaway insects; Aunt Chrissie says straight after dinner she will get to those sleeves and lengthen them. At this Philip smiles, the old smile that Alvie can handle. Draining her glass, she catches his eye and tosses him a black, giddy simper. A tic jumps at the corner of his mouth.

"Chrissie," he says — he directs all his comments at Aunt Chrissie but keeps glancing at Alvie. "Chrissie, this is a survival thing, did you know that given a choice, in a maze say, slaters will turn right then left then right then left?" Well gee whizz, Phil.

It is arranged that Philip will take Alvie sightseeing. Alvie sees Aunt Chrissie give Uncle Rupert a pleased little nod. Philip takes her first to the museum, a sombre great building with a tarted-up cable tram at the entrance. Alvie's brain grows muzzy as Philip yaks on happily about the model steamships and the cutaway trains. They look at Phar Lap in a glass case. Phar Lap's coat gleams and muscles ripple as though he wants nothing better than to burst through the glass and gallop out of that winter-still room. Philip explains that his heart which was more than twice the weight of that of a normal horse is displayed miles away in the national capital. Alvie looks from the dead gleaming horse to Philip and sees that little tic jump again when he catches her watching him. She wonders if he has ever kissed a girl. When they come out at last into the spring sunshine which has cast a sherry-coloured glaze over everything, she takes hold of his hand, and keeps hold of it all the way home in the tram.

Back in the Jennaways' garden, she tells him she has something to show *him* — and she takes him through the tangled prunus and flowering currants to the platform constructed in the big leaning wattle. "My old treehouse!" he says wonderingly. "I made it years ago out of some bits of timber left over from something but I can't recall playing in it much." Climbing up, he leans down to give her a hand but she laughs and pulls herself up. Twigs catch at their hair. They sit down. She puts her arm around him and, leaning her head against his jumper, listens to his heart busy in its own secret world. "I don't like cold dead places with old dead horses without hearts," she mutters.

"What did you say? I can't hear you."

For reply she raises her face and runs her tongue over his ear. He shudders, his lips touch hers. He tastes nice, she decides, better than Butch Gilbert or Herbie Mason who mash your face with their demanding smoky tongues. After a while she sits away. "Let's leave some for tomorrow," she says faintly.

The next day, and the next, and the next, they hurry home from the art gallery, Myer's bargain basement, a second trip to the museum. When his tentative hands have gone far enough for that day according to the code of the girls back home, she draws back and asks him things about himself. Get them talking, says Cass Jawkins, it gives you a breather. But Alvie surprises herself by actually listening. Back home she never listens to Herbie or Butch. Philip says he doesn't know much about girls. He envies her, going to a mixed school. There's a girl on his tram but he doesn't know how to start off and anyway it doesn't matter now, does it? He envies people like Chrissie and his father, and now the Skerritts, some people are just lucky, able to love, he was coming to believe he was one of those people destined to miss out on all that.

What a screwed-up life! Alvie feels a pang of affection for that boring, bossy, jostling family back home.

"Does your mother have a boyfriend?" she asks one afternoon.

Philip shrugs. "She's always going to the theatre and things with people — men — but she says they're all pigs. I guess that means me, too. She's joking of course but you know what? She used to complain if Dad so much as came into the bathroom when she was having a shower."

"What was he trying to do? Pinch her bottom?"

"Maybe."

At this incongruous view of Uncle Rupert, Alvie laughs. She has a quick picture of herself: soap up to the chin in the old crazed bathtub at home, and in bursts Gorgeous to pinch her bottom — who? David Bowie? Prince Andrew?

"Aren't you glad I'm not one of your museum pieces, Phil?" she asks, nudging him.

She is not prepared for what happens next. It's as though some crazy kid has thrown himself into Uncle Rupert's leather armchair and flung it over backwards. "I could rape you, you know!" he blurts. As she twists her head angrily, thinking What a dumb thing to say, he throws himself off her, crying "Help me, Alvie! I don't know what I'm doing, I'm so crazy for you — I feel ashamed but why should I feel ashamed, you don't, do you? But then you're not a rapist, are you? My mother reckons a fellow that does that to a girl against her will deserves the knife." She would, thinks Alvie. "Maybe we'd better stop coming here — yes, that's the only thing, Alvie, stop coming here, stop kissing, stop going around together to museums and things."

Alvie sits up and brushes twigs and wattle bloom off her coat. "Aunt Chrissie will think we've had a fight," she says slowly. It's as though someone has copied out the right formula and passed it to her under the desk. She says, bending down to him, "Do you really want to? Stop coming here, I mean? They haven't planned anything for us for tomorrow, Phil." And watches her hand run over those forlorn shoulders until he turns to her, saying "You know I don't!"

"So . . . no more attempted assault, huh?" she jokes, but her voice sounds strange, dazed. Tomorrow she will know as much as anyone — her mother, Cass Jawkins. "Only you'd better get something," she continues. "You know — get something? Glad Wrap, that'll do." So Cass Jawkins reckons.

But next morning she wakes with a familiar drag in the pit of her stomach, a heavy, fat cramping, and hurrying to the bathroom to make sure, she flies into a rage against all those forces — Butch Gilbert, Cass Jawkins, her own body — that are pushing her into this thing with Philip and then at the last moment like a stupid joke shoving Charlie in the way.

Perhaps Philip won't want to today, she thinks — perhaps he's forgotten — but no, when they set out at Aunt Chrissie's suggestion for a picnic in the botanic gardens, he turns aside at the Jennaways' front gate and pushes through the shrubbery to the treehouse. Savagely she thrusts away his hand and climbs up by herself. "Philip," she says, and now she is nearly crying, Alvie Skerritt caught cheating at last. "Listen, about us — there's *Charlie*."

"Charlie?" Philip frowns, drawing away. "Charlie?" At this reaction Alvie is offended. Because it's something that happens to half the world, isn't it? Just because *he* doesn't, he needn't back off as though she's diseased. She is so angry that she fails at first to take in Philip's hurt protest: "You didn't tell me — only of course there would be, wouldn't there, lots, I suppose, queues — droves — I guess I was just an amusement."

She is too busy saying caustically "Charlie's not my

favourite friend, actually. Nor anyone's." At this point she realises Philip's mistake, and laughs. Philip says "Actually I don't much like two-timing myself," and tries to shake off her hand when she takes hold of his arm.

"Relax, relax," she soothes, much as her mother soothes her father when he's tensing everyone up about bombs or green belts or something. "I can't help it, truly I can't." She takes a deep breath. (A female has to make the most of these things, Alv.) "That Charlie gets around — more than you ever will, Phil. He's what you might call unavoidable amongst the girls I hang around with."

"All of them?"

"All of them. Sooner or later."

Without another word Philip jumps down from the treehouse. Then, because he is a courteous boy brought up to help women, he turns back to assist Alvie. But refuses to look at her. So this time she takes his outstretched hand, and, when she is standing on the ground again, sways against him. Puts her arms around him. Observes the familiar tic begin to twitch at the corner of his mouth. As soon as he kisses me, she tells herself, slipping her hands under his jumper, Just as soon as he kisses me I'll tell him what Charlie really is. Her hands move up and down that resisting back. But he has to kiss me first.

OUTSIDE THE SILVER DORY

Near the head of the queue outside the Silver Dory there was a man carrying a half bottle of riesling.

"I've been looking forward to this evening all week, haven't you?" he said to the two small boys accompanying him. He was the only person in the queue who did not shrug deeper into his collar as the wind lifting from the sea whirled a fine sand along the pavement and into people's faces. Instead he kept rising on his toes and glancing around, at the lengthening queue, at the group of boys throwing a frisbee under the Norfolk Island pine by the jetty, at the waiters who with closed intent faces were making a final check of the tables inside the restaurant.

"Doesn't it look good in there?" he said to his boys. "I wonder which table will be ours. This one in the window, do you think? I do like the red tablecloths with the white napkins folded in peaks, don't you? And did you notice the waitress has red stockings to match? Perhaps she'll be serving at our table. It's all very tasteful, isn't it? Nothing pretentious. Look at those nets hanging around the walls, and the big glass floats, and the crayfish baskets —" The boys' eyes darted like fish in a net as the voice swept over them. "Crayfish grilled with garlic butter — yum! I bet you've never had crayfish with garlic butter, eh? They're called lobster on the menu but they're really our very own local crayfish. Did you know crayfish have to moult in order to grow? I'm going to have whole grilled green lobster with garlic butter . . . mmm, yes."

"I thought lobsters were red," ventured the elder boy, the one carrying the bottle of apple juice, as soon as his father drew breath.

"Will there be hamburgers?" asked the younger boy.

"Fish and chips?" demanded the elder. "That'll do me."

"There'll be lots more exciting things than fish and chips," said their father, delighted. "This *is* going to be a good evening. What do you two say to letting me choose something you've never had before? What about blue swimmer crab, or grilled flounder caught this very morning while you were still asleep, and served up whole with parsley and tarragon and dabs of butter?"

"I read about a boy who choked to death on a fish bone," said the elder boy.

"Harvey Smith went to McDonald's with his dad the other day," said the younger boy.

" — and no one noticed what was happening till it was too late."

Their father almost sprang off his toes with pleasure. "But chaps, obviously his dad wasn't there to show him how to tackle unfilleted fish! It's all a matter of knowing how to go about things the right way," he explained. "Not long now," he added, glancing once again at his watch and then fondly at his boys. Seeing them hunch their shoulders and turn side-on to the wind, he almost flung his arms around them and hugged their bird-frail little bodies to him. "Did Mummy forget an extra jumper?" he couldn't help saying. The elder boy grinned up at him and wriggled away. "Bet you anything that frisbee lands in the water, Toby," he boasted to the younger boy.

The man dived on this new subject as though it were the frisbee itself. "Some of the men where I work go across to the park and throw a frisbee around every lunchtime — grown men!"

The boys looked up eagerly. "Do you do that, Dad?"

He shook his head. "Too busy." And he set about explaining to Derek and Toby, just as he had many times in the past, first to their mother and latterly to Donna, how you had to keep on your toes if you wanted to get anywhere in his organisation; no, not only get somewhere, simply hold your place in the line. And the closer you were to the top, the harder you had to run. As he talked his gaze stretched across the emptiness between himself and the brilliant city; what by daylight was the friendly old bay busy with dinghies and fishing boats and ferries was by evening a solid unlit void. The red eye on top of the Harbour Bridge snapped at him mockingly. "How can a void be solid?" he wondered aloud.

The boys shuffled, then dropped their heads to watch the waves beating on the upturned dinghies moored to the restaurant's sturdy verandah posts.

"This place is going to fall down soon, I reckon," Toby said cheerfully. "It's not new and shiny like that McDonald's where Harvey Smith went with his dad, is it, Derek?"

Their father laughed. "No Toby, I don't think it's going to fall down soon." Then he sighed. "These days some people are just a bit too eager to chase after the meretricious. Do you know what that big word means, meretricious?" The boys heaved their shoulders and rounded their eyes. "Actually, Toby, this is the best fish restaurant in the city — along the entire south coast. It's not what you'd call posh, that's pretty obvious, but there's plenty of atmosphere as you'll feel as soon as we get inside."

"Gee there's plenty of atmosphere out here, I reckon," joked Derek, pulling his jacket up on to the top of his shoulders against the biting wind, and looking to his father to laugh. But his father didn't laugh. He hadn't even noticed.

"No, it's the quality of its seafood that's made the Silver Dory famous —"

The boys saw a one-cent piece on the footpath and began scuffling over it with their feet. Derek cheated, hooking Toby's leg with his so that Toby lost balance and clutched at the ample backside of the woman in front of them. "They use old-fashioned methods that don't damage the catch —" their father was saying, and found himself addressing an indignant face with waggling chins that in his startled imagination blossomed into all the furies of nightmare. He made himself smile at something, anything — the outdoor tables and chairs stacked under the window until summer, the tops of the boys' heads, the line of would-be diners that by now had reached almost to the intersection. Young, old, in couples and in small groups, still people came hurrying. "You have to be early if you want a table at the Silver Dory, Derek," he commented to the elder boy, since his last remarks had been directed to Toby, and he made a point of being scrupulously fair.

"You have to be early if you want a table at the Silver Dory, Toby," repeated Derek, letting Toby win the one-cent scuffle, and casting an admiring glance at their father for being head of the line, or almost. Unconsciously he began to imitate a little mannerism of his father's, rising on the spot from heel to toe, heel to toe. It was a habit of the man's that had made the boys' mother want to scream, so she used to tell him.

"Don't fidget, Derek," said the younger boy bossily, with a self-conscious smirk at his father.

"There's no one else like us, a dad taking out his young sons as far as I can see," the man observed, craning his neck. He took a deep breath. "When I told Donna where you and I were going she was quite excited," he continued carefully, watching them out of the corner of his eye. Neither boy said anything. What Donna had actually said was "The Silver Dory! Now that's a place I've always wanted to go to, Maurice." As he recalled her tone of voice the boys' mother chimed in, not speaking to him, of course, but loud in his ears nevertheless: So where did he take you this time, boys? Well, well, well . . . I suppose I'll hear nothing but Daddy this and restaurant that for the rest of the week! . . . "She would have liked to come too, you know," he said, fingering the neck of his half bottle of riesling.

The elder boy punched at something imaginary above his head.

"Mind that apple juice, Derek," said the younger boy.

"Yes mind that apple juice, Derek," said their father. "I know you two are going to enjoy drinking apple juice with your fish much better than that Fanta you'd set your hearts on," he added. "Fanta is much too sweet to drink with seafood. Look, I've brought along a bottle of riesling, Clare riesling, that's a fresh, crisp, dry wine that goes down well with lobster or fish." The boys looked up at the word Clare because that was their mother's name. "Well, a half bottle as you can see, because I'll be the only one drinking it." Seeing that he had regained their attention he flung himself into that other business, the business he had intended not to tackle again until they were all three comfortably seated, their stiff table napkins unfolded, their drinks unstoppered by the red-legged waitress, the boys chattering about marbles or Mummy or whatever boys chattered about. "Chaps, you remember that little matter we were discussing earlier today?"

"About why you didn't come to Derek's football match on Wednesday?"

"No, not Derek's football match." He smiled down fondly at Toby. "I mean that other matter you and I were discussing." The boys flicked a glance at each other. "You know, when I first got Mummy's letter about that, I felt very angry. *Very* angry. At first. But then, after I'd thought about it for a while I began to see Mummy's point of view. And I think she was right. Mummy was right. Wouldn't you agree?" Across the dark expanse of the bay a cluster of lights was moving, a fishing boat, perhaps, setting out for the next day's catch, its mast and decks picked out with glowing bulbs of light and cutting steadily through the darkness. "Wouldn't you agree?" he repeated.

"Me and Harvey Smith nearly got a try," said Derek.

"Harvey Smith's dad took him to eat a Big Mac afterwards," said Toby.

"Gee Dad, wish you'd seen me nearly get that try!" shrieked Derek. Ha, changed the subject that time, didn't we, Dad! his expression seemed to say. He glanced at Toby, triumphant as any breakaway flinging himself over the touchline.

Around them they felt the entire queue stir, surge forward a little. Through the glass panels of the restaurant door a waiter in black coat and stiff white shirt front and ready-for-all-of-you smile could be seen approaching.

The man had a fleeting fantasy of himself and the boys and the boys' mother all together at the table in the bay window — the boys engrossed in the novelty of the menu, the oysters slipping and sliding down his throat, the woman, one wrist on the table, the other curled in her lap, leaning attentively towards him — an image so fatuous that he forgot it instantly as the door was thrown open.

"My word, I *am* looking forward to this evening," he repeated as they climbed the worn stone steps. "I think this is going to be one of our best evenings together, don't you? A really successful time all round. Wouldn't you say?"

PIETÀ

Rome . . . he says, spinning the globe on his desk another section. What do you want to see in Rome?

Jeez, breathes Vivie, her face lighting up under her funny blue hat. *That* far?

He laughs. Vivie, as yet unsure about his laughter, bites the nail of one mittened finger. It's a habit he is trying to wean her of, along with an initial wariness, and certain oddities of dress that he puts down to youthfulness. Leaning across his great desk he takes first her hand in his and then her face and kisses her. The white telephone on his desk rings, stops, starts ringing again but he goes on kissing her.

He takes Vivie to Rome in late summer, squeezed in between two conferences — just in time for the last of those great big peaches! Vivie exclaims, pointing. He laughs again. Is Rome to be peaches, then? — Rome, where at every step, every turn of the head one can feast on man's rendering of the sublime? Nevertheless, each morning before breakfast he hurries out of the hotel (and Vivie hurries sleepily after him) to a market close by in a side street, a succession of stalls on barrows where vanilla-eyed Romans urge them to buy great bloody steaks, holy pictures, rolls smoking hot from the bakery.

He buys Vivie's peaches from an old, old woman with a

medallion of the Virgin at her throat. He asks in his stilted Italian if he may pick out the fruit himself. The old woman is charmed at his effort. *Si Signor!* Vivie's mouth waters at the sharply sweet odour of peaches. Her eyes cling to his hands as he selects each fruit, turning it over slowly, slowly, so that she thinks it too must become alive to his touch. Making herself use a perfectly ordinary voice, jocular, tart even, she says to him, Come on, what's the hold up, *you* wouldn't build Rome in a day.

As they walk back to the hotel, her hip nudging his every third or fourth step, she remembers with a small shock of triumph how that toothless old stallholder also was gobbling up his hands — or maybe she was just counting peaches.

Leaning against the door of their room, he pants a little with the effort of walking up three flights of stairs. (It never occurs to Vivie that at his age he might prefer the lift.)

You're greedy! he laughs.

So are you! she retorts.

I know, he says, delighted. I get greedier every day.

And afterwards, peach juice dribbling down her chin and on to her breasts, and the discarded furry peach skins flung shrivelling into the wash basin, she sighs, Do we *really* want to go out sightseeing?

He laughs. Go and have your bath.

Go and have your bath, he repeats as she dawdles, just to hear him tell her again.

When at last she is bathed and dressed, and has filed and painted her nails (she has given up chewing them), and splashed herself generously with her new perfume, she finds him looking through the art book he bought her. Michelangelo, he is saying. One of the greatest artists of the Renaissance. If not the greatest. Look at this, Vivie — can you imagine the mind that could perceive such grieving in a lump of stone?

Beats me, Vivie laughs, to please him peering over his shoulder. And she feels a surge of excitement that takes in everything, her decision to toss away her old life like a too-tight hand-me-down coat, the fun time he's giving her, the pizzas and the chianti, the cadence of tongues, the quick little Italian cars dodging right up on to the footpaths —

At the kerbside he says, Don't hesitate, just step out on to the road, the traffic will go around you. And so it does. (Just as he said it would back home when she thought she was trapped on a kerbside of habit and indecision.)

With him, she ceases to be nervous even of the gipsies on the Metro steps, those big swarthy women in voluminous black who crowd around shouting *Buona Fortuna!* He is her good fortune. At his suggestion she carries nothing in her hands. Even her comb she slips into his pocket. For a few days she tries carrying some Italian *lire* in a body belt, along with her passport and air ticket, but the body belt looks bulky under her new summer clothes, and is so awkward to get at that after a few clumsy efforts she deposits the lot in the hotel safe and leaves it to him to see to everything. I'm not going to lose you! he laughs, as she hesitates over the passport. We'll settle up later if that's how you feel about it, he says, amused. Oh I do! she insists, but in the lazy heat of Rome she keeps forgetting to buy a notebook and pencil and jot down her share of expenses.

It adds up to the same thing in the end, he tells her. Golly he's cluey! she scrawls on a postcard to a girlfriend back home. Vivie is full of admiration for cluey men. For instance, this one has long ago devised a method of coping with the pitiful beggars they come across everywhere. Each day he gives generously, very generously, to the first beggar they see — the blind man by the station entrance, the cripple, the man with the placard stating simply *Ho fame* — and after that nothing more to anyone that day, no, not a cent, no matter how much they whinge or wheedle. Better to fork out a decent sum once than have your hand in your wallet all day long, he explains. It adds up to the same thing in the end.

Glancing back covertly at the day's beggar, often she catches a look of surprise opening around stumps of teeth into a fawning grin. And Vivie walks on thoughtfully.

They go, of course, to St Peter's. Waiting apart from the crowd in the Metro while he queues for train tickets from a vending machine, Vivie glimpses a young woman moving purposefully from person to person in the queues. Her feet are bare, and she is wearing a long faded skirt, and a scarf knotted at the back of her head. She is not as dark or as big as those women in black crowding the Metro steps, nor as fair as the Romans — an Arab, maybe? He would know. From her manner Vivie thinks she's doing something political, handing out pamphlets or presenting a petition or something, things people of Vivie's age always seem to be doing, but as she approaches his queue and Vivie sees him reach for his wallet, she realises that it's just another beggar, their first for the day. The woman is carrying a baby along one arm. She stops beside him, speaks. Vivie sees him give. Smile. But the woman does not smile in return, does not lift her eyes or drop them in a show of gratitude, simply tucks the money away somewhere inside her clothing and moves on.

And then, as though this has been her intention from the moment she hurried down the Metro steps on her thin purposeful feet, the woman moves across to where Vivie is waiting, and in a weary voice makes what sounds less like a request than a demand. Vivie catches a couple of words — *la medicina,* baby, the woman says — in English, as though she knows who Vivie is, knows the threadbare life she has run away from, sees those guarantees of independence, purse, passport and air ticket, stashed away in the hotel safe, sees the very room where every morning Vivie sprawls gobbling peaches.

Glancing from the thin, unsmiling face to the child lying slack on her arm, Vivie sees on its neck and hands and feet horrible pustulating sores painted with some red stuff, Mercurochrome it is called at home. Forcing herself not to flinch, she tries by exaggerated looks to convey her concern, then by gestures that he has given for both of them, given generously, *molto, molto. Mio marito*, she stammers, pointing with one scarlet-tipped finger first at him, then at the funny old ring that he likes her to wear. *Mio marito* — But the woman will not understand. A hard look comes over her face and, pointing to her sickly baby, she makes a low impassioned speech, the gist of which is perfectly obvious to poor Vivie.

All she can offer is the metallic phrase, *Mio marito!* My husband, my husband! At last he has finished at the vending machine, he is approaching, putting his wallet safely inside his coat and quickening his pace as he observes the woman. *Se ne vada!* he says sharply, and then, as she hesitates, *Vai! Vai!*

She didn't realise you'd already given her something for the both of us, Vivie says, clamped to his side as he hurries her down stairs and around corners. I should've given her something myself. That little kid looked real dreadful. Of course she might be just a fraud — not her kid at all — buying drugs — and what good could *I* do except make myself feel better —

Does it matter? he asks gently. Their platform roars and shudders. In the scramble to get on to the train Vivie's final wail is lost: But I'd like to have had the chance to decide for myself!

Such thoughts must be jostled aside in the crush to get into St Peter's. Covering her head with the new silk scarf he has brought in his pocket for this purpose, he makes a passage for her up the steps, through the great bronze door and into the biggest church in the world. Vivie gasps. So much gold! So many statues! The great dome rising up, up like a cry, and behind the altar, brilliant as sunrise, a throne where Vivie half expects to see the Pope at least.

Tourists are everywhere, craning and murmuring. Look! Vivie whispers, nodding towards some women in saris, and then towards a party of dark-suited Asian men busy with camera flashes. Yes, people come from all over the world, he says proudly, as though it is his very own work that he is displaying to her. He repeats names — Giotto, Bernini, Michelangelo, Basilica — and to Vivie they sound like a litany to which she doesn't know the responses.

Jotto! Is that some new game? she mumbles, scuffing along behind him.

Ah! At last! he cries. What did I tell you this morning? . . . If you look closely you will see his name carved on the sash across her breast, Vivie, he points out.

Oh you men! she mutters, head down, eyes fixed on her sulky feet. Always wanting to leave your mark on things! What did *she* want?

Good God! he exclaims. We're talking about Michelangelo! We're talking about marble! He lowers his voice as an attendant in black looks their way. There'd be nothing but a great block of stone if it weren't for the artist, Vivie —

He's like a kid, Vivie thinks. He's just a great big kid, with his games and his bossing and his stories. An old geezer rabbiting on about some other old geezer.

The old geezer is saying wistfully, He was only twenty-four when he completed it, Vivie. Only twenty-four!

The sudden change in his tone touches her. Lifting her head she finds herself looking at another woman who wasn't given the chance to decide for herself, but in a blaze of light, or stars, or angel's wings, found herself lumbered with a kid. And she loved that kid, she was good to him, and what happens? A pack of yobbos run nails through him and break his legs and when he finally conks toss him back into his mother's lap.

Light glows through the veins and folds and angles of the painstakingly worked stone until it is living flesh that Vivie is gazing at. Through a haze of tears she sees a young woman in a gipsy scarf, one arm supporting the man, the other reaching out to Vivie in a gesture of recognition and pity.

A SEA STORY

Around the blood and bones and nerves of the man stretches the skin of the holiday house. It was her idea, not his,
this beach place like time itself suspended in the tree tops
and falling step by log step down the cliff to the ocean.
From the balcony there is such a tangle of lillypilly and
cycad that he can't catch even a glimpse of the ocean. She,
of course, is delighted. "Perfect!" she tells him, everything
as usual staked up with exclamation marks. "Heavenly!
Isn't it? Thank goodness we decided just to drop
everything!"

He grumbles — says springing things on you like that
means there's no anticipation, no forward planning. "So?"
she replies, not really listening, grabbing together her
bathing things even though they've only just arrived and
nothing's unpacked and has she checked there are safety
flags?

Every night, after they make love, she sighs once then falls
deeply asleep. But he — he feels the rasp of sand on the
roof, the rumble and push of the surf like a meal that won't
settle. Every morning he wakes exhausted. The smell of
frying fish assaults his nostrils. She thinks because you're

at the coast you ought to eat fish; she takes an extravagant, childlike pleasure in all the different ways she knows to prepare it. She thinks you should catch it yourself, too, but when they try from the jetty with all the expensive new gear she impulsively bought him for Christmas, all they haul up are two minute bony whiting and one fair-sized leatherjacket. She is very excited about the leatherjacket until she starts to clean it and out crawls a pallid thing with legs like a giant louse. They watch it trying to pick its way across the sand towards the water lapping against the piles.

At least, that is how *he* remembers it. She says she remembers it differently, they weren't down at the wharf when she cleaned the fish but back at the house, and the thing didn't crawl anywhere, just waved its legs a bit inside the fish. That's how it was, she insists, surely he remembers, herself kneeling over a pile of newspaper by the back steps and him looking down from the verandah. "Come out there now to joggle your memory," she says. "If it's bothering you."

He stares. "How you do go on! But if it's bothering *you* . . . " They almost quarrel. Then — "Nitpicking," he tells her, and bites back laughter. "Horrible!" he says, changing tack. "That fish looking perfectly normal and all the time that — that *thing* inside it — "

And hears her say, the knife bloody in her hand and the leatherjacket slit open at her feet, "I expect we only caught it because it was sick and slow." And sees her take it by one fin and toss it to the greedy, squabbling gulls hanging around the wharf. Then, turning to him, "All gone," she says, mock-motherly.

That is what he remembers. That is how he has filed it.

After that he insists that they buy all their fish at the marina.

*   *   *

He hears the whistling kettle screech. That means breakfast is ready, she is about to fling scalding water into the teapot. In a moment she will troop in to wake him. She does. She comes right up to the bed and whispers his name. He winces. His eyes climb open. She puts him in mind of some exuberant puppy waiting with a stick in its mouth for a game. She has presumably been up since daybreak, hiked along the ridge to see the kangaroos as she likes to do, then plunged into the ocean for her pre-breakfast swim that she insists gives people a good healthy appetite. A good healthy appetite: what a packet of buzz words!

"Everything's ready," she smiles, looking at him not, he suddenly realises, with the malleable eagerness of a domestic pet but with the gaze of some curious wild thing glimpsed from the edge of dream.

She has had her shower and now as she kneels on the edge of the bed her robe falls open and her breasts jump out at him. Juices flow stinging under his tongue. In her groin little tendrils of hair curl damply like ferns in rain forest. "Table's set, everything's ready," she tempts him. He could lose himself in this wilderness and what staff clerk thumbing through the files would so much as recall his name?

"I thought we were on holiday," he jokes. And does not move.

There is a tiny pause. "So did I," she rejoins. His body jars as she pushes herself off the bed. In a moment he hears her clattering about in the kitchen again, refilling the kettle, singing even; he smells burning toast. What a creature of chaos she is! Force of habit at last drags him out of bed and under the shower. It is a tiny cubicle near the back door. He adjusts the taps quickly, huddles under the faucet. Steam lulls him. He sways from side to side and lets his mind make patterns: soap and soap holder; hot tap, cold tap; his towel, her towel; in tray, out tray —

"Don't forget there's just one small rainwater tank, dear," he hears. She is outside the shower recess; there is only the thin skin of the curtain between them. His thoughts fall apart, grow loud, shudder and shriek at him. He flings himself out of the shower; buries his face in the towel nearest to hand and is enveloped in a musky clinging smell: hers, he has seized her towel in his panic. She is as inevitable as the sea.

Dressed, combed, shaved, he finds her in the kitchen. She has already eaten her share of fish; on her plate the skeleton lies exposed and discarded. His portion is keeping warm over a saucepan of hot water on the stove.

"I'm going for a walk," he mumbles. "Work up an appetite."

He plunges straight into the bush, ignoring the possibility — the likelihood — of wolfish ticks skulking on the underside of the dusty grey leaves of the tea-tree. Ancient cobwebs full of dried leaves and insect wings clutch at his face; his expensive new running shoes bought to jog around the park back in the city each lunchtime fill with grit and twigs. All at once he comes out of the scrub on to the edge of the cliff. At his feet is a large flat rock that he recognises as one that juts out from the cliff top. He has seen it many times from below when scrambling around the rocks at low tide. And now he hears, he feels the roar and shock of the waves. His feet are on the rock itself, they carry him right out to the edge. Peering over, he sees that the tide is in. The sharp teeth of the rocks are bared as the water draws back to make its rush at the cliff. Great dark patches of kelp lift and tug. A tongue of foam slavers. Spray leaps towards him, climbs up, up, only to fall back and gather itself again.

A movement in the corner of his eye startles him. He turns — ready with a dozen glib reasons why he should be leaning out over a sheer drop like a lover from a balcony.

But it is only a kangaroo, watching him with soft drowned eyes from the tea-tree. For a moment man and beast stare at each other, then he shouts "Hoy!" — and again "Hoy!", laughing to himself as it crashes away. When once again the morning is loud with silence and the endless pattern of the sea, he edges gingerly off the rock and turns back towards the house.

As though she knows these things by instinct, she has his breakfast ready the moment he reappears — not fish after all but what he always has at home, grilled tomato and egg and a rasher of bacon, three slices of light toast in the rack, and a fresh pot of coffee. He takes up his knife and fork eagerly. All that is missing is his morning paper. The long day stretches ahead but while he is occupied with eating he won't think about that.

AT THE SIGNORA'S

The Signora never advertises, yet every summer guests fill the red-tiled stone farmhouse easing itself gently down the Tuscan hillside. Perhaps it is the hazy, delicate light of late summer that they come for; perhaps it is the novelty of staying in a real olive grove — in spite of its being rather neglected these days — and breakfasting on the saltless bread of this region, fruit fresh from the Signora's garden, and quark, a special curded cheese that the Signora insists is quite different from the German quark.

From miles away they come, in big cars barely scraping through the narrow medieval streets, like the Schumachers, or winding up from Florence by bus, like the Bradleys, and lurching the last few kilometres to the farmhouse in the Signora's old Fiat. "We are your family of nations!" someone exclaims, Herr Schumacher probably, peering in the dim light of the entrance at the Signora's guest book that she keeps on a table, along with guide books and maps in a variety of languages, left over from previous guests.

Some guests arrive on foot, like young Drew who is hitchhiking his way around the world. He says he hasn't had a haircut since leaving Australia and he's not going to have another until he returns. His hair stands up around his head in wads of curls — wasted on a boy, Frau

Schumacher laughs. She has such a girlish, expectant face that when she says things like that even Drew joins in her laughter.

Frau Schumacher and the Signora find much to say to each other. The washing-up water in the stone sink greases over and the weeds under the olives grow higher as they converse in part-German, part-Italian, each talking so loudly that surely neither can hear the other — but what does that matter? When she first arrives the Englishwoman Mrs Bradley, who speaks neither Italian nor German, tries out her rusty schoolgirl French, "Savey-vous planter la pamplemousse?" but no one is listening. Frau Schumacher tells the Signora about the Schumachers' son Volkmar who is studying for an important exam, and the Signora tells Frau Schumacher about her husband the professor whose work takes him to Sicily. He is so happy in Sicily. He was born in Sicily. My husband is not of this country, explains the Signora. Frau Schumacher likes to ring Volkmar every evening, she tells the Signora, just to see how he is getting along. She feels a little bit bad about having a holiday while her poor son is working so hard. The professor works hard, says the Signora, her voice growing louder and her eyes flashing. See all the things he has brought back from his work! And they look around the room at the crowds of books, papers, paintings, jugs, pinned broken plates, shards of pottery, figurines, a great terracotta oil cask, and the shafts and tailgate of a peasant's cart so brightly decorated you can almost hear the farmer and his sons and daughters singing as they return from the fields.

The professor does not return often to the farmhouse in Tuscany, says the Signora sadly. It is the Signora's farmhouse. She grew up in it. She, like it, is of this country: Tuscany. Now it is sliding down the hillside like a rheumaticky old farmhand. Schumacher laughs at Frau Schumacher for ringing Volkmar so often — you think he is a little boy in short trousers, Mrs Schumacher? — and Frau Schumacher laughs at herself. But he is a Sicilian, that is it! shouts the Signora, her greying hair flying around her shoulders. He is not of this country! Every time he returns to my country he brings something else from his work. Soon there will not be room for one more broken plate, another old tailgate!

Maybe he stops coming then! laughs Frau Schumacher.

If Frau Schumacher is always chuckling at something, Herr Schumacher is full of jokes. They are not very good jokes, certainly, but because they are all on holiday everyone smiles. "*Molto grazie!*" say the Bradleys to the Signora, practising a phrase out of their Berlitz pocket book after a particularly satisfying breakfast of bread, coffee, cheeses, meats, figs, blackberries, honey and four sorts of jam. To be sure the bread is as hard as a rock, because the Signora is convinced that it is bad for the stomach to hoe into today's bread, which arrives with tantalising yeasty smells in a little van at daybreak. But that is just another of the Signora's eccentricities; no one really minds; it is all part of the pleasure of holidaying in an olive grove in Tuscany. So — "*Molto grazie!*" mouth the Bradleys. "*Molto finito!*" caps Herr Schumacher, his hand on his heart. And everyone laughs.

While the weather lasts breakfast is eaten outside on the patio. Herr Schumacher is usually first to be seated at the old wooden trestle table under the ilex; the others dawdle upstairs, writing up diaries or postcards, or gazing at the view out the bathroom window. "I'm giving a lot of thought to our projected joint paper," fibs Dr Bradley to a colleague on the back of the head of Michelangelo's David. (At the postcard stand his wife, inattentive as usual, was on the point of buying a close-up of David's genitals.) "Today I'm setting out once agen," Drew scrawls in his dogeared diary. "Tho it's tempting to stay on & do nothing, just lie in the olive grove & forget about how things are out there." "Dear Volkmar," writes Frau Schumacher, who has mislaid her biro so has to push hard on the nib of Herr Schumacher's gold fountain pen that he never lends anyone. Mrs Bradley, writing a poem in her head, lingers under the shower until a pool collects on the bathroom floor and she has to swish it away with her sandal. Drew, glancing over the balcony in case breakfast is ready, sees Herr Schumacher at the table and adds "I don't try to discuss enything so I get on fine with everyone here tho the German bugs me, I can't stand these heel-clicking types." Then he throws his diary into his rucksack, pulls on his *No Nukes* t-shirt and clatters downstairs, because surely by now the Signora is ready to come running with the pots of fiercely strong coffee that is the signal to eat?

There is no sign of the Signora, however. Not liking to seem impolite to someone older than his father, even old Schumacher, Drew sits down at the other end of the table and nods man-to-man. Herr Schumacher, who has been studying a road map, pushes his reading glasses to the end of his nose. "So . . . you are leaving us, Drew? Once more you set out on the big adventure?" he says, with a glance at the rucksack with the blue and white Southern Cross inked on to the flap. Drew nods. "Ah yes, it is wonderful the things young people can do today," sighs Herr Schumacher, something Drew has heard many times on his travels, like a faint rebuke. "What a pity you did not tell the Signora sooner that you leave this morning," continues Herr Schumacher.

"How's that?" asks Drew, but before Herr Schumacher has time to explain the others appear, Dr Bradley automatically taking his wife's elbow although she looks as fit as he to cross a few cobblestones unaided, and Frau Schumacher exclaiming as she lifts her hands to the day, "Schumacher! Today we go to Pisa, *ja*?" To each in turn

Herr Schumacher gives a little bow, putting his hands on the table and raising his elbows to show he would stand if he could. "Dr and Mrs Bradley! Good *mor*-ning." He pronounces the name carefully, *Brrrad-ley*, so that Mrs Bradley, pleased, finds herself blushing as she slips on to the bench beside him. "Mrs Schumacher! Good morning to you, too. I trust you slept well?" continues Herr Schumacher. Frau Schumacher laughs her husky, purring chuckle. "I am saying to Drew what a pity it is he did not tell the Signora sooner that he leaves us this morning. She makes always a special dinner when a guest is leaving," he explains to the Bradleys who are more recent arrivals at the farmhouse.

At this mention of the Signora everyone looks hard at the covers still laid over everything on the table. Where *is* the Signora? The morning is slipping by, already the church bell on top of the hill has pealed out — jangled — as though boys on their way to confession have tugged a demure schoolgirl's plait.

"The Signora cooks — how do you say it? — something particular of this region," explains Frau Schumacher, with a glance at her husband whose English is so much better than her own. He nods, so she continues "Beef —"

"Fattened to a special procedure in the valleys —"

"I've seen nothing but olives and grapes around here," puts in Drew. "Maybe it's really Australian beef, imported."

"Kangaroo?" And Dr Bradley laughs at his own joke.

"In the valleys higher up," continues Herr Schumacher. "Fattened —"

"And cut thick, *so*," adds Frau Schumacher, indicating with thumb and forefinger. "And cooked on the big open fire in the sitting room."

"But it must be with olive wood, nothing but olive wood."

Drew says he's a vegetarian most of the time.

Frau Schumacher says she nearly is, too, after the Signora's special dinner to say goodbye to the Danes, the night before the Bradleys arrived, the meat cut *so*, and cooked a little little bit on the outside, what is the word, burned? singed? and all the *Blut* — the blood — running out on the plate and getting mixed up with the lettuce. She has to pretend she has too much on her plate and pass it on to Schumacher.

"My wife likes to eat meat if the meat is well cooked," explains Herr Schumacher.

"*Ja*, and if I cannot see the form of the animal — the thigh of the hare, those quail in France with the little heads looking up from the plate — you remember, Schumacher? Brrr!" Frau Schumacher shudders, and laughs so merrily that the two retired farmhands who have rooms at the back of the house in return for helping harvest the olives, look up from chopping something on a wooden block under the clothes line.

"I guess everything's okay so long as we can't see its shape," says Drew, in a tone that makes everyone stare.

"They say it's somewhere around here that Leonardo tried to fly," Mrs Bradley interposes hastily, before their silence can harden.

"His assistant actually, Muriel," corrects her husband. "A young lad. He crashed, of course."

"Of course!" Drew continues. "Who else? Not the inventor — never the inventors of these things but the assistant."

"All the same it would be rather delightful to try, wouldn't it, in such a lovely lovely landscape?" cries Mrs Bradley in a high false voice, at Drew's words frightened for all these young people sent out on foolish adventures. "The grape vines you would see crisscrossing hills and valleys, and the children running to school, and in the distance the great towers of Florence."

"Some hunter would get you," Drew interrupts. "Haven't you noticed how few birds there are around here? Compared with Australia, anyway," he adds, to no one in particular.

Frau Schumacher folds her arms on the table and leans towards him. "I think you are a little bit homesick, Drew?"

Her Schumacher laughs. "My wife likes to ring our home every day."

"Last night after dinner we speak to our son," says Frau Schumacher. "Speak? Speaked?" ("Mrs Schumacher! Mrs Schumacher!" groans Herr Schumacher.) "Last night we telephone to our home and we spoked to Volkmar. I think he would be happier out on the road like you, Drew."

"It is a good day for travelling," says Herr Schumacher, and they follow his gaze past the unpruned olive grove, up to the town and beyond to the cypresses, stiff as soldiers along the skyline.

Someone asks Drew about his prospects of getting a lift south quickly. It transpires that about his destination Drew has not yet made up his mind, not definitely, not finally he tells them, it depends on a few things, a phone call to friends in Hamburg, but probably he won't be travelling south, travelling homewards, but north, to meet up with these same friends in Hamburg to take part in the peace demonstrations this coming autumn.

"A contradiction in terms, surely?" smiles Dr Bradley. " 'Peace' and 'demonstrations'?"

Not at all, says Drew. There will be no violence. Everyone will have some training beforehand in passive resistance. He and his friends will form a support group for one another. That's what being friends is about, isn't it? If anyone starts acting afraid, or aggressive, or both, the others will lead them aside and talk them out of it. And it will work. Because the demonstrators are only putting into practice what everyone really wants. Isn't that true?

(The others nod, oh yes, it's what everyone *wants*.) Of course he thinks about going south, about going straight home, it would be so much easier, but this is something that has to be done. *Someone* has to.

"When I was your age," says Herr Schumacher suddenly, "No, younger than you, I was at school in Dresden. It was wartime, you understand. As soon as we were old enough my whole class joined up — twenty-one of us — you know how it is, at that age, you think it is the thing to do, it is a big adventure. So off we all went. To Normandy. Five of the twenty-one returned alive."

"And not much of Dresden left, either," remarks Drew.

"You know about Dresden? How do you know about Dresden?" Herr Schumacher looks delighted. "It is so long ago — before you were born — and so far from your country. Yet you know about Dresden!"

Drew hesitates. "My grandfather was a prisoner of war — but no, that's not why I'm interested, I hardly knew him really, no, I just think about things, maybe we should all think about them —" He reddens, seeing the others exchange glances, but makes himself finish: "Dresden was *people*."

Herr Schumacher says excitedly, "I too was a prisoner of war! I was captured by the Americans at Normandy. Lucky for you I was not killed, heh, Mrs Schumacher? Instead I was for many months lying in hospital. While I am recovering they discovered I have a facility for language, *ja*?" He beams. They all nod vigorously. "So after I am mended I spent a year in the prison camp as interpreter for the American camp doctor. Ah, he was like a father to me, that man. I was not yet nineteen, you understand. A mere boy! And when at last I returned to Dresden I did not recognise it, no street, no home, no parents, nothing. Only as a memento of my big adventure, this —" and thrusting out his chin he shows them a jagged scar running under his jaw and disappearing into his collar.

"There was an uncle in Hamburg —" prompts Frau Schumacher, as the others begin to fidget, faced with they know not what ugliness patched together under the neatly pressed shirt.

" — and so I went from Dresden to Hamburg, otherwise today I would not be here and I would not have met you, Mrs Schumacher."

"Yes, it's a terrible thing to be an occupied country," sighs Dr Bradley.

"My friends in West Germany certainly think so," says Drew fiercely, determined to tear at the lazy Tuscan morning so that clear light can burst through, the harsh cleansing light that he yearns for. But the others are no longer listening. They are thinking about breakfast. A surprisingly late riser for a farmer, the Signora knows that this particular day everyone wants to be off early, to galleries that open only in the mornings, to Pisa while the Tower is still standing, to the crossroads for a lift before summer disappears in a cloud of acid rain.

"Her car isn't where she leaves it by the gate," someone observes, craning. "She must be up in the town."

"Talking. Talking. That's the Signora's gift — conversation." And they smile. But they are getting awfully hungry.

"Maybe she has gone to the bus stop to meet her husband."

"*Is* there a husband?"

"Of course. The house is full of his things."

They fall silent for a moment, thinking of this shadowy husband who spends long months in Sicily while weeds spring up under the olives and the Signora warms herself with conversation.

"Maybe she has already prepared the coffee for us," suggests Herr Schumacher, sliding past Mrs Bradley so that he can go in to see.

Yes, the coffee pots are bubbling nicely but is the coffee ready? Is it too soon? Better wait for the Signora, says Herr Schumacher, walking up and down the patio and jerking his elbows back to stretch his shoulders.

"Oh I do hope it's a bit weaker today!" murmurs Mrs Bradley, knowing she will not dare ask again because when she said something that first morning the Signora flashed "Huh! You like *English* coffee?"

At last they hear the Signora's car. It is unmistakable. It backfires up the drive, jerks to a stop on the patio. Out jumps the Signora, hair flying, hand to her heart. "Sorry — so sorry — I will quickly bring coffee and then something I have to say —" head bobbing, smiling so apologetically from one to another that for a moment each guest feels uneasy. It was Schumacher's nightmare, I should have wakened him sooner, thinks Frau Schumacher. It is Muriel's long showers, thinks Dr Bradley. It is my big car, worries Herr Schumacher, thinking about his old uncle's business that provides for this annual vacation, himself at the wheel now and his wife beside him in her new crocodile shoes . . . Sometimes as we drive through these little towns children, watched by their parents, fling stones as soon as they see the number plate . . .

Mrs Bradley is watching some imaginary spot in the distance that is forced to descend because of the danger of hunters, a tiny winged figure zigging and zagging to dodge their shafts until he floats peacefully the last few yards to land by the Signora's breakfast table. Mrs Bradley moves up to make room for him (or his assistant, was it?) and of course it is only Herr Schumacher sitting down again, someone less like Leonardo she can't imagine. She glances at him sideways, this German old enough to have fought against *us*, and sees a bead of blood where he has nicked himself shaving.

Only Drew is unconcerned by the Signora's words. Already he has said goodbye, already he is out on the highway, rucksack on his back, rain biting into his neck and shoulders — "We've been talking about World War Two," he says as the Signora whips the covers off the table.

"Ah *war*," cries the Signora. "Do not talk of such things!" She gives him a quick hug, riffling his hair. "Your own mother and father were just children then. Have you not happier things to think on, *carissimo?*"

"I wasn't much affected by the war," reminisces Dr Bradley. "I was too young, and besides I was sent into the countryside where things were comparatively safe. But that was a long time ago! If you talk about 'the war' today young people think you mean the Falklands."

"I spend the war not here on the farm but in Firenze," recalls the Signora. "It is not a good time — no, I cannot speak of it. But this I tell you — in 1944 while our young boys are fighting the Nazis who are in how do you call it? retreat, the Americans are in the Palazzo Pitti on the other side of the Arno doing nothing but watch to see who will win."

"Oh I say!" protests Dr Bradley, who has read the military histories, and understands the logistics of battle.

"This I see!" shouts the Signora. Heads shake. Ah, these nations. America! Germany! Easier to throw stones at a passing car forty years later than keep in mind a boy with shattered bones. The Signora goes on, "They watch and we see them watching through field glasses from the Palazzo Pitti — but no, more I do not want to remember. You go south, Drew, in the south it is warm."

"*Ja*, south," says Frau Schumacher. "It is good for families to be together."

"And today he sets out," smiles the Signora. "So! I have a surprise for everyone. That is what I wish to say. Since it is his last morning with us —" and from the car she brings with a flourish a delicious-looking cake, a slab of sponge covered with grapes baked reddish-gold in their own juice. To be eaten with quark, she says, quark of this country. Frau Schumacher describes the delicacy of German quark and in a moment the two women are laughing and shouting at each other, a barrage of jocularity.

"Give my love to Sicily! My heart is in Sicily!" cries the Signora, as Drew takes leave.

Only Mrs Bradley feels certain that he will go north. "We send our children to fight for us while we sit here in the sun . . ."

"But is not that always the way, Mrs Brrrad-ley?" says Herr Schumacher gently. "Well, Mrs Schumacher, are you ready? Pisa! Pisa is like a woman, she leans but she never falls," he jokes. He makes them laugh again, pulling a droll face as he says "Today I will ask for tickets for two children and see what happens. *Ja.* I have tried that before, I say Tickets for two big children, please — but no one believes me."

"He would make the Mona Lisa laugh," says Frau Schumacher.

Everyone smiles at that, too.

While the two women help the Signora clear the table, Dr Bradley, claiming no respite, lights up his pipe and in a haze of tobacco smoke spends two minutes, even three, contemplating his joint paper. Soon Mrs Bradley, losing herself in her poem, wanders to the back of the house where, covertly admired by the two old farmhands, she stares into the tomatoes as she waits for the very word.

Frau Schumacher waits for Herr Schumacher.

Herr Schumacher, watching Drew getting smaller and smaller as he walks up the hill beside the olive trees, suddenly says "Before we go to Pisa, Gisela, don't you think you should telephone Volkmar?"

"But Heinrich, last night I telephoned Volkmar."

"Yes Gisela but that was yesterday. Today is today. Don't you want to be sure that everything is all right? You put the call through, I will come in when he answers."

And Herr Schumacher goes on watching the vanishing figure of Drew.

HARVEST

It's New Year's Day again. Joan Skerritt has the food packed and the little kids hurried up, Ray Skerritt is out in the garage turning over the motor, and still young Alvie is mooning around in her nightie. All at once she announces that she doesn't want to go to Grandma Lafferty's this year. *Because*, that's why! She won't go!

All right, she'll go.

She puts on her old pink singlet instead of the blouse her mother has ironed especially, a 1940s puce skirt with the hem coming down, and her razor-blade earrings.

You're as cranky as all-get-out sometimes Alvie, they complain. Not go to Grandma Lafferty's! But everyone does — all the Skerritts and the Jennaways and Aunt Trudi Lafferty. It's New Year's Day!

Big deal! Drawing her knees up under her chin so that her feet aren't hooked around the esky, Alvie flings herself into the corner of the back seat as far as she can from hot, fidgety little Trish squashed between herself and Billy. Oh to fly past her father's head through the open window into the blankness of the sky! Once she used to enjoy the idea of a new year; she would skin off the old year like a tatty shirt and finger the new one like something she had saved up the deposit for. Not any more though. She drops her head to her knees and, rubbing her forehead against the grainy material of her skirt, shuts out the rest of the world as she breathes herself in.

"Sit up, Alv, you keep falling on top of me," Trish sighs.

"There'll be an extra one in the back coming home, don't forget," Ray Skerritt reminds them cheerfully. Sitting up at these words, Alvie stares into the back of his head as though it is her mirror at home and practises that special flaunt of the head until her earrings jangle.

Billy leans forward past Trish. "You got toothache? Alvie?"

Grandma Lafferty lives in the last house in a street above the bend in the river. It is an old house, weatherboard, set amongst shrubs and perennials. Pink and crimson roses in a second burst of bloom clamber over the gateway, and a huge apricot tree with gobs of fruit still clinging shades the verandah overlooking the river.

Joan's sister Trudi Lafferty arrives at the same time as the Skerritts. As they walk around the side of the house to the back door, country fashion, Alvie overhears her aunt say to her mother, "Isn't it funny, Joannie, as soon as you're back at the old place it's as though you've never stepped a foot out the gate." Joan Skerritt laughs. "Never — but always about to!" And thrusting the littlest girl Lurlene at Alvie she swings around on the spot like a girl herself as she takes everything in again. *Never but always about to*. Wacky, thinks Alvie. The sort of thing Philip Jennaway likes raving on about, discussing he calls it. He's been sending letters to Alvie since the August school holidays, every few days at first, now every two or three weeks. *Never but always about to*, that's a dickbrain idea, she tells him. Dumb. Wet. Pathetic. Screwed up. And she launches into another of those replies she writes in her head and never sends.

They all troop into the kitchen, Trudi and Joan first because they've raced ahead like two kids, then Alvie carrying Lurlene on one hip, the little kids Trish and Billy, and finally Ray Skerritt with the picnic basket and the flowers and the eskies.

"Well now!" says Grandma Lafferty, taking stock of them one by one from the stove where she is stirring something in a large pan. "Well now!"

Joan Skerritt and Trudi Lafferty begin to flutter. "Good grief, Mum! In this heat, Mum! On New Year's Day!" Billy shrieks "I'm as big as you now, Grandma! Grandma!" and Grandma Lafferty ruffles his hair and says "Well now!" Turning to the others she draws each grandchild to her, saying things like "Here's the little rosebud" and "Ooh I could gobble you right up" and "Very bright, very bright today, lovie" — this last to Alvie.

Alvie, glancing at her mother, swishes her skirt triumphantly as she takes a deep breath. The kitchen is full of a sharp, sugary smell that all at once is reassuringly familiar. It is the smell of all the New Year's Days that she can remember. Spatters of toffeed fruit cling to Grandma Lafferty's apron; the old woman explains that she is just running up a spot of apricot chutney from the last of the fruit off the old tree so they can all take some back with them; she meant to do it yesterday but it was too hot, a real stinker, today's cooler thank goodness. This chutney's good-oh (lifting a dollop on her spoon and dropping it back into the pan), it goes real well with a bit of cold mutton, she thought for lunch they'd have just that, fresh chutney with cold meat off her weekend roast, she got an extra big leg especially, that's if one of the men will carve, Ray, or Chrissie's husband when he gets here —

Alvie sees her mother and aunt look at Grandma Lafferty's red face, at the simmering pan. "But Mum," they soothe persuasively, as though they are dealing with somebody's obstinate child, "Wouldn't tomato sauce do just as well?" And they become awfully bossy, it seems to Alvie, sending Trish and Billy outside to play, urging Grandma Lafferty to put her feet up — like two kids playing at grown-ups, Alvie thinks, with their own mother as the little girl.

"I'll carve, Grandma," she volunteers loudly.

"Bless you, lovie, but that's a job for one of the men," her grandmother replies. And rumbles in her throat with fond laughter.

Before Alvie can think of something to say that is both polite and enlightening, Aunt Trudi intervenes. "If that's so then I'm doomed to be a vegetarian," she says, winking at Alvie. Grandma Lafferty, mashing a chunk of pulp against the side of the pan, says sadly "No Mr Right yet, then, Trude? Just other people's children all day in the schoolroom?" In the midst of what sounds like the same argument mother and daughter have been having for years, Aunt Chrissie and Uncle Rupert Jennaway arrive.

Alvie's skimpy singlet feels suddenly tight. Philip is with them. Of course he is. He's to come back with the Skerritts this evening to stay for a while. It's all arranged. No one has asked Alvie what *she* wants, Chrissie has him every holidays and last August she had Alvie as well so it's only fair says Joan Skerritt. Do the boy good to see how the other half lives says Ray Skerritt, he can come with me and look through the paper mill. You've never taken *me* through the paper mill, Dad. Did you ever ask, girl? No — did Philip?

Joan Skerritt adds as an afterthought, You two kids got on all right didn't you. The way she says it, it's not even a question.

Oh sure. We got on all right didn't we Phil.

. . . You took me to see that old cable tram and Phar Lap and Aunt Chrissie got out an old school magazine with one of your poems in it and you'd never kissed a girl until I kissed you, you were the shyest boy I'd ever gone around with but even so that lunchtime in the arcade you couldn't stop kissing me and Gog and Magog nearly scared us to death striking half past one and you said you'd never been so happy in all your life and that really did scare me —

As Philip follows Aunt Chrissie and Uncle Rupert into Grandma Lafferty's kitchen Alvie sees that the tic at the corner of his mouth is jumpier than ever, the thin wrists more restless. He glances eagerly at Alvie, then looks away so quickly she has to pretend she's all smiles across the kitchen at Grandma Lafferty's chutney jars. Chrissie Jennaway pushes him forward. "Mum, you remember Philip, don't you? Rupert's boy? He wasn't with us last time." Philip comes towards Grandma Lafferty, hesitates, then holds out his hand. "How do you do, Mrs Lafferty?" He is Aunt Chrissie's stepson, not a proper grandchild at all, but Grandma Lafferty draws him down to her and kisses him just the same. "Everyone calls me Grandma, lovie." At this Philip smiles, the smile that lights up his whole face, and Alvie thinks, Just wait till Cass Jawkins and Susie Fisher see *that*. Now Philip is smiling at Alvie. She widens her eyes, rolls one shoulder. Philip, caught along the blade of those flashing earrings, snatches up a chutney jar and examines the rim.

"How's it going, Rupert? Ray?" The brothers-in-law shake hands. "Looks like the women have got everything under control in here, eh?" "How's the state of the nation, Ray?" Rupert asks drily. "You probably won't agree with me on this, Rupert, but I reckon if the government doesn't — " Ray Skerritt is away. As they move across the room to get a couple of beers each from one of the eskies, he says to Philip, "Cheer up son, we'll all be dead soon," and then, as though to make clear this is only a bit of Skerritt chiacking, no harm meant, he thrusts a can at Philip, claps an arm around his shoulders and sweeps him outside.

Well, thinks Alvie crossly, All those letters and not even hello! Sometimes, wading through Philip's letters, she gets the feeling he is simply talking to himself. "I don't think one can properly appreciate Art without some experience of Life oneself," is the sort of thing he writes. "And at the same time Art renders that experience more real. For example, reading *Sons and Lovers* as we are this term —" Well gee whiz Phil. Even those other bits, the bits she marks in red texta to read out to the girls at school, sound as though he has rehearsed them, and she pictures him, alone with that mother of his in the big empty house where he lives during term time, scribbling and crossing out and listening to each phrase in his head.

Grandma Lafferty's girls have taken charge of the chutney, ladling it into jars, wiping things, writing labels. Seeing Alvie hovering, Aunt Chrissie suggests that she take Grandma Lafferty out to the verandah. "Take Lurlene too," Joan Skerritt adds. "Mind she doesn't fall down the steps," calls Aunt Trudi. "Who — Lurlene or Grandma?" Alvie shouts back sarcastically.

As she settles her grandmother into a deck chair she exclaims "You shouldn't let them push you around, Grandma."

"Me? Push me?" Grandma Lafferty's rumbling laugh boils over. "It's all right, lovie." She leans forward suddenly, leans over Alvie all breathy like that Cass Jawkins at school. "They do me real proud, those girls of mine. Turned out real well." She gives Alvie's knee a shake. "If only we could find the right one for poor Trudi, eh?"

Alvie jerks her knee away, shrugging deeper into her deck chair as the three men, talking together, crunch past below the verandah. "All this fuss about boyfriends, where does it get you?" she snaps, reddening at her tone of voice to her dear old grandma.

But Grandma Lafferty doesn't seem to notice, just goes on rumbling the way old people do at their private fancies. She lifts Lurlene on to her lap, where the little girl plays with the heavy watch that used to be Grandpa Lafferty's, just as Alvie remembers doing, sitting out here on New Year's Day in these very same deck chairs and listening to an anecdote about young Joannie or Chrissie or Trudi — "real cards, those three!" Alvie pictures her mother twirling in the garden, *Never but always about to*, scary somehow. Her mind grows heavy and slack. Wind idles through the leaves and along her skin like the murmur of her grandmother's voice. Apricots grown out of reach ooze sweet overripeness, or fall with a soft thud into the shadows. Below, where the garden ends and the ground falls away, the river flows like sleep.

Now Grandma Lafferty is talking about the apricot tree. She tells Lurlene how it grew from a stone someone must have tossed over the verandah, and as the seedling grew up she wouldn't let Grandpa Lafferty pull it out, no she wouldn't, this wild thing that had sown itself right next to the house and grown into a fine garden tree, its branches cool and leafy in summer and in winter pencilled thinly across the night sky.

"And the blossom, I even picked some this year, there was so much," Grandma Lafferty is saying. Alvie sees vases, milk bottles, buckets massed with pink flowers, and a bee straying unnoticed. "And then one morning I looked out and I could see the tiny little fruits, they were suddenly there, dozens of them. I always enjoy watching the fruit grow. And then, of course, the birds came." Well that's all right, isn't it, thinks Alvie dreamily — wild birds to a wild tree? "What a job, shooing those pesky parrots! A peck here, a peck there, never the same apricot twice. Shoo! shoo! shoo! all day long." Alvie, protesting, flees in rainbow flight with the bright-eyed squawking rosellas. "But all the same, the tree was loaded this year," Grandma Lafferty continues. "Apricots to eat, apricot pies, apricot jam —" Mushed into jars with lids and labels! cries Alvie. "A bonza crop this year, did me real proud . . . He likes you a bit, hey? That young man?"

Alvie's eyes snap open. Her grandmother's face has gone sly again. She is glancing down into the garden and back at Alvie. The girl jumps to her feet. "I'm going for a walk, Grandma," she says abruptly. "Lurlene'll be just fine with you." And she plunges down the verandah steps and along the path that leads to the river, running, running in a panic of protest. She should never have come! Shrubs catch at her hair, the sky claws at her. Then everything becomes ordinary again as she sees her father and Uncle Rupert and Philip, and she makes herself slow down to a saunter. They are leaning against Uncle Rupert's new Saab, talking politics still, she hears, strolling closer. It's clear Philip doesn't know much about politics; he probably doesn't even know her father is shop steward out at the paper mill. The unions cause a lot of the trouble, Philip is saying, all those strikes just before Christmas. Ray Skerritt isn't contradicting this, just nodding slightly and saying "Is that so?" — saving it all up for the next couple of weeks, Alvie guesses, grinning inwardly. Uncle Rupert's not contributing anything either, but you can see that he's listening anxiously; he wants his boy to shine.

"Come on, Phil, let's go for a walk," she interrupts, self-possessed again, rescuing him before he can say something too stupid.

"Dad'll be raving on about disarmament next, bet you anything," she says, leading him between borders of pinks and heart's-ease and forget-me-not towards a broken paling in the fence. "Just you wait till he's got you at the table at our place."

"Just as well I came along when I did," she continues as

Philip says nothing. "They looked like Gog and Magog getting ready to strike, didn't they? . . . I suppose they're still there, Gog and Magog, I mean." Holding the broken paling aside for her, he gives her one taut glance. Then, as he goes ahead automatically, ready to help her scramble down the steep bank, she shouts "Cat got your tongue, Phil?"

He turns so suddenly that she collides with him. "Why didn't you answer my letters, Alvie?" *Answer my letters, hand in your homework, get home before midnight . . .* As she stares at him, making her eyes very round, he bursts out "Seven lines on September the twenty-ninth, five on October the tenth, and last week your Christmas card! That's all." He doesn't remind her that for Christmas he sent her not a Woolies card picturing snowmen and santas like hers to him, nor his usual stilted letter, but a poem, a short, spontaneous poem of his own making that she hasn't dared show a soul. At least, she supposes it is a real poem — she understood most of it first go so she has her doubts. Sometimes she thinks it is the most beautiful thing anyone has ever given her, and sometimes she can't bring herself to read more than a line or two because it's so private, it's like spying on people in parked cars, he's making her look in the window of a parked car and the girl inside is herself. Before he can talk about the poem, ask her something hard she can't answer, she says quickly, remembering all those replies in her head, "I'm not as good at letters as you, maybe, but I wrote scads, every day sometimes, truly I did."

"Did you? Did you really?" He frowns. "Perhaps they got lost in some strike."

"I guess that's it." She watches a coke tin drift towards her, turning slowly as it is carried level and then past until it is no more than a glint in the slow brown water.

"I thought — I was beginning to think you must be angry with me."

She sighs impatiently. That's how it is with guys like Philip — they want to take over the girl's share. "Are *you* angry with *me*?" she counters.

"*Alvie.*" The nerve at the corner of his mouth is like an insect trying to escape. "How could I be?" And he tells her again, just as he told her over and over that last night of the holidays — Aunt Chrissie and Uncle Rupert only two bedrooms away, herself thinking Now I'll know as much as anyone, Mum, Cass Jawkins, then biting her wrist so as not to flinch and Philip crying "Alvie! Alvie! Do you want me to stop?" though neither of them could have stopped by then, and afterwards shaken, not quite believing, but pleased, something to tell that Cass Jawkins back home she was thinking, and Philip in tears with wonder or relief — over and over he told her "I never thought anyone would love me so much."

Hearing him say it again she feels claws of panic.

"Listen," she says suddenly, "You know what the school counsellor said to me a few weeks ago? She said, You've gone all quiet this term, Alvie, what's wrong? You're not pregnant, are you?"

"But you said — you were sure —"

" — and I said, No of course not, Miss McHugh, I've just had my period. And *she* said, Well you shouldn't even have to say that, Alvie, should you?"

"Then you have been angry," he says at last.

"Not angry. Scared," she says. And sees that he doesn't understand at all, how could he, she hardly understands it herself. It's not the usual things, scared of getting pregnant, scared because some smart teacher has caught you out, no, it's something much more subtle. You can't wait to read a red texta bit from his latest letter to the other girls but when you see Cheryl Whitrod grinning sideways at Susie Fisher you switch in mid-sentence to a page and a half about Art and Life so that they all groan "*Bor*-ing!

Jeez, Alvie!" and you shrug and fold the letter away, too bad. And that's weird. Scary.

Philip is saying "Tell me what you mean, Alvie. Is it me you're scared of?" and then, "Maybe you'd rather I didn't come back with you this evening. I guess I'd better go back to Melbourne with Dad and Chrissie."

Neither looks up as Trish and Billy, thongs in their hands, streaks of mud on their legs, rush past shouting "Hurry up, you two — Grandma'll make us wait lunch for you!"

Alvie frowns. "Thinking about other people," she says. "That's what's scary . . . That's what I've been telling you, in all those letters you never got."

"Tell me now, then. Tell me, Alvie. I can take it."

She smiles wryly. Take her dealing him out to the others under the old gum tree at the end of the oval? Poor old Phil, it would kill him.

"Forget it, Phil," she says gently, catching hold of his hand. "I'm starving. Let's go back to the house." As the anxious, tight looks goes out of his eyes, she thinks He's *gor*-geous! He hasn't changed a scrap. Wait till the others see my cousin from Melbourne!

Hurrying back for their lunch Philip says "And now I'll tell you something no one else knows about yet. I've had a poem accepted by a magazine."

"Wow! Your school magazine?"

"No, much better than that, a poetry and prose magazine for people under twenty-five from all over Australia. It comes out quarterly and my poem will be in the next issue."

"That's great, that's really great, Phil." She stops abruptly. "You don't mean — not *that* poem?"

He nods shyly. "You liked it, then?"

And now she really is scared. "Yes of course, but — now everyone will know."

He shrugs. "I don't care. I'm not ashamed of how I feel. Why should I be?"

"I'm not talking about just you!" she shrieks. "Don't you see, the others will guess, your father — Dad — Aunt Chrissie's probably telling Mum right now! Telling Grandma! Jeez Phil, how can I ever go in to lunch!"

"Alvie! I just told you, no one else knows about it except you. It's not even published yet."

"But it will be." He's being about as smart as someone who doesn't draw the curtains in a panel van. "I don't go around telling people about *you*!" Oh sure, she has read bits out of his letters, and she boasted to Cass Jawkins "So what's all the hassle, the next day I didn't feel any different" and that's true, but the poem is truer: is Philip, is herself, oh how *could* he betray her? "Ask the magazine not to publish it, Phil."

"Fair go! My first acceptance!"

"Yes but — telling everyone like that —"

"No one will know it's about you," he pleads. "They'll think I'm just daydreaming again."

Me and him, she thinks. Him and me, no one else and then he goes and uses that time we had, uses me . . . "It makes me feel sort of . . . *used*," she says slowly.

He turns on her. "Don't *say* that, Alvie."

"I thought you wanted me to tell you things," she retorts. "I thought you said you could take it."

"You sound just like my mother sometimes," he says after a moment. "She's always on about how men use women, *always*, she means. I hate listening to her, I begin to believe I'm all those awful things she says men are. That's why it was so good being with you at Chrissie's, and going around Melbourne together, and then that last night — You're right, I'd better go straight back home."

He turns and walks away from her up the steep incline into Grandma Lafferty's garden. What's his mother got to do with anything? she asks herself. I'm not his *mother*.

"Phil! Wait!" She runs after him, seizes his arm so that he has to stop. "Go and put your case in our car."

She feels a flutter of jubilation as once again she sees the tension fade.

"Really? Are you sure?"

"Sure."

"And you do like that poem, don't you? You do like it?"

She laughs, forgetting for the time being those qualms about publication. "Well I have to, don't I? It's about the only poem I've ever been able to make any sense out of."

He scoops up an apricot stone from the path and hurls it towards the river. "People don't understand poetry just by reading it, right? Right."

Before she can reply one of the women comes out of the kitchen, calls over the verandah rail "Hurry up you two, everyone's waiting," and dashes inside again.

"Never but always about to," says Alvie, and laughs.

Then, although she feels another moment of panic as she realises Grandma Lafferty is sitting on the verandah look-ing down on them, knowing, satisfied — or maybe she is just dreaming of apricots — Alvie throws her arms around Philip then seizing his hand runs two at a time up the steps for lunch.

A SENSE OF PLACE

(I) International

Con walks in the early morning streets of Pretoria and wishes she had her camera. Now white, now black, the separate groups throng past. Typists, she guesses. Bankers. Factory workers. *Polisie*. Here comes a black girl carrying a bottle of coke on her head; slender as the neck of the bottle and as steady glides she.

Con walks in the early morning streets of Pretoria and looks at people's faces. Curious white men with heavy necks eye her sideways. Black people drop their eyes. A black man accidentally brushes against her and veers away. "I am so *sorry*, madame!"

Now Con is upset. She can't bear such deference, she wants to wrench it from him and hurl it back in his teeth.

She hurries back to the hotel. Walter and Paul are already in the dining room.

It is an international hotel, that is, it is now permitted to take black guests. Con looks with interest at the two black people who are seated at a table nearby.

Walter says "If they can afford to stay here they probably have American accents."

Breakfast at the hotel is delicious — sweet tropical fruits picked that morning, *matabele* porridge, guava juice.

When her stomach is full Con is no longer so angry.

"What shall we look at today?" she asks over her second cup of coffee.

(II) Them

Con asks "Do people eat goat around here?"

"No."

"That's interesting. In Nigeria people eat goat's meat."

"Oh! The *blacks* probably eat goat."

(III) Mangoes

People are very hospitable. Con is invited to stay in a country town.

One afternoon after lunch she finds herself sitting by the open sunny window in the van Winkles' living room, explaining herself to the head of the house while in another room his wife packs his overnight case.

"Do speak louder, Con," she calls. "I don't want to miss a thing."

Con in mid-flow about Canberra as compared with Pretoria can't help smiling: back home there isn't one of her friends who would still pack for her man.

"You are going abroad?" she asks suddenly, politely, sensing her host has stopped listening.

She tells herself it's his home, his country, she shouldn't feel niggled if he switches off.

"Oh no," says Piet van Winkle. "I am going to Capetown. Overnight."

"I have no wish to travel outside this country," he adds. "I can see all that I wish to here."

A black maid called Happy appears with coffee on a

tray. On her back, in a blanket, sleeps the van Winkles' baby. "She just loves that little kid," Carolyn van Winkle says. Con wonders how many children Happy has had to leave behind in one of the distant Homelands. So, still niggled, as she takes her cup she smiles thanks up at the silent, shut woman, smiles *you can look at me, I understand, I really do,* but the maid's eyes refuse to meet hers.

Drawing herself up straight Con tells herself Before I leave I'll make sure she smiles. And for a moment, until she realises what is happening, what she is doing, she repeats She *will* smile, she *will!*

Out in the street two African women are engaged in loud, cheerful conversation, not in English, not in Afrikaans — Zulu or Sotho perhaps. Piet van Winkle frowns. "You know, that's something I can never get used to. They pass a friend in the street and they continue the conversation for a hundred yards — shouting." He stands up. "I'm afraid it annoys me."

Snap! The window is shut, the venetians closed. Sunshine and voices fade away. He goes out to the kitchen and fetches himself a mango which he eats carefully, slicing it with a knife and paring close to the stone.

He doesn't offer Con a mango.

(IV) Them

At the international airport, two young women suddenly turn to Con, and without any preliminary explanation or identification whip out a sheaf of papers and ask how long she has been staying in South Africa, and why. Surprised, she hedges "Do I have to answer this? Why are you asking all these questions?" "No of course not!" says the first girl, snapping shut her briefcase while the second says sarcastically "Because we just love interrogating people!" And they turn away huffily.

"Relax, girl," Paul says to Con. "They're just a couple of chicks doing a survey for a government tourist agency."

"They could have said so."

"The face of nameless officialdom," Walter pronounces.

"*Them*," says Con, but her comment is drowned by the loudspeaker announcing their flight from Pretoria to Perth.

PIECES OF FURNITURE

Old Mrs Ryan, standing on the step of the back porch, watched her son and daughter-in-law carry a window frame across the lawn towards the garage. She could hear Harold saying to Elsie who was creeping backwards, "Sod it Elsie, try letting your arms drop, *drop* I tell you!"

Mrs Ryan's breath snagged. "He needs his cup of tea, Mr Magoo. Harry needs his mum to get a nice cup of tea."

After weeks of silence it was the third weekend in a row that Harold and Elsie had dropped by. Mrs Ryan knew this for certain because whenever Harold came to visit she coloured in the date on the kitchen calendar with a red texta. Catching sight of those fat red squares gave her a good feeling. A family feeling.

Two weeks ago Harold and Elsie had arrived with a trailer-load of furniture, a few bits and pieces Harold had said, well a dining room suite actually that he'd like to stack in his sister Vera's old bedroom. Last weekend they had turned up with some lengths of timber. These Harold said he wanted to store in the old wooden garage. "But Mr Magoo uses the garage, Harold," Mrs Ryan had said, her veins suddenly hurting. "Mr Magoo sleeps out in the garage." Mr Magoo was a moody part-Persian cat with a flea collar and a bell. Right now, leaning against Mrs Ryan's shin, he seemed as puzzled as she was with Harold's and Elsie's comings and goings.

They saw Harold and Elsie come out of the garage again and, each taking hold of one of the rickety doors that had stood open for years, lift them closed. When Harold and Elsie stood aside they saw, attached to the door bolt, the padlock Harold had brought with him last time. "Now why does he do that, puss?" muttered Mrs Ryan. "I didn't ask for a padlock." She watched Harold coming towards her, a big man pushing impatiently at the apples and pears overhanging the path. "I'll ask him about that padlock just as soon as he gets inside," said Mrs Ryan. But at that moment something happened that put the question right out of her head. Walking past the garden tap that dripped constantly on to the path and made a pretty green moss grow between the cracks and over the slabs, Harold skidded and nearly fell. He had to grab at the tap to save himself. Mrs Ryan heard him swear, foul words his father used to come out with just to shock Mrs Ryan when they were first married. Wheezing, she hurried into the kitchen to put on the kettle. "I'm all thumbs today," she told Mr Magoo. She had to strike six matches to get the gas going, and even then she scorched her fingers.

"Finished, dear?" she asked, putting her hand over the dead matches as Harold came into the kitchen.

"For Chrissake Mum, you might break a leg out there and no one would know, the place is so damned overgrown," her son replied, bending down to kiss her.

Mrs Ryan thought of reminding him that there was no need to shout, she could still hear perfectly well, but said instead, "Yes, those old trees could do with a good prune . . . I used to do them myself," she told Elsie. "But these days I don't seem to have the strength in my hands that I used to." She glanced at Harold's big hands.

"These things do happen, Mum," Elsie said, reaching for the cups hanging on their hooks in the dresser. "Old people on their own falling or having a heart attack and not a soul knowing for hours. Days even. You read about it every day in the papers."

"I don't," said Mrs Ryan, feeling a familiar pinching in her chest at Elsie's words. She glanced reassuringly at the bottle of white pills that she kept next to the junket tablets. "I don't because I've cancelled the paper."

"There you are then," said her son. "Not even the paper lying around on the front lawn to warn the neighbours that something's wrong."

"It's good of you to worry about your old mum, son," Mrs Ryan said. And for a moment she saw facing her not the middle-aged man, grey, balding, softening into fat, but the young man, her boy, that scallywag who was all over the neighbourhood, the little nip Harry who vowed he would always take care of his mum and young Vera. There was no Elsie hanging over the front fence then! The neighbours said Mrs Ryan spoiled Harry but what did they know? "What are you doing?" she turned on Elsie who was splashing about in the sink. "I washed those cups this morning — those plates too."

Elsie, smiling apologetically, went on scratching with the pot scourer. "Just a little bit of grot," she smiled. "The light from this kitchen window isn't the best, is it, Mum?"

"It's done me for near on forty years," retorted Mrs Ryan. Her shoulders began to prickle. Elsie's smile was like wearing nylon on a hot day. "I like this house," she went on, her chest squeezing again at the thought that these two were up to something, getting her to move in with them maybe, or into one of those cramped rooms in some old people's home. "Mr Magoo likes it here, too. He wouldn't be happy anywhere else."

"So long as you're managing, Mum," smiled Elsie.

Reassured somewhat, Mrs Ryan nodded. She didn't let on that with some things she wasn't managing — the washing, for instance. Little things were all right; she could do them in the handbasin and hang them over the side of the bath. And she wasn't as silly as she once was about all this changing so often. But when it came to the sheets and towels . . . she could still manage the machine (just) but reaching up to the clothes line had her stumped. Each time she tried she started to black out. She had to dry them indoors over the backs of chairs. Rather than think about that, she continued "I've lived in this house half my life. I brought up two kids here. It was tough in my day for a woman on her own."

"Yeah yeah yeah," Harold said. "Elsie —" He flicked his head towards the front door. Elsie shook her hands free of soap suds and wiped them on the tea-towel.

"But aren't you staying for a cup of tea?" wailed Mrs Ryan, frightened suddenly that she had put them off by too much talk about the old days.

"Just a few more things to bring in, Mum," Elsie said soothingly. "We'll be right back."

Mrs Ryan thought she meant something from the car, a few fresh vegies maybe, or a nice bunch of flowers. But shortly, hearing them moving about at the front of the house, she went along the passage to see. A fly buzzed in through the open front door. She could see a pile of furniture out on the verandah, and propping the door open, a dressing-table that she couldn't bring herself to look at. Under one eye her cheekbone began to throb. She turned away into the second bedroom, the one Vera used until she got married and went to live in the country.

Harold was in Vera's bedroom moving things around again. As well as Vera's furniture, with the vase of flowers that Mrs Ryan liked to keep fresh on her desk, there was all the stuff Harold had brought two weeks ago — a table top leaning against the wall, table legs laid across the bed, and lined up in front of the wardrobe, six dining chairs with cushions. Mrs Ryan stared. Their leafy pattern that she herself had chosen was black now with years of other people's grime.

"Getting pretty chock-a-block in here, Mum," Harold said cheerfully. "The rest of the stuff will have to go somewhere else. We'll try my old room."

"But I've got all I want in there already," Mrs Ryan protested. The words echoed in her head. Hadn't she said the very same thing two weeks ago about Vera's bedroom? "Your room's very nice as it is. I don't need any more furniture, Harold."

"Yes but like I explained last time, Mum, now the old man's dead I need somewhere to store his things. Remember?"

Mrs Ryan frowned. Funny, she could recall clear as daylight something that happened nearly half a century ago, yet what she had said a fortnight or even a week ago had already grown muzzy. Diffidently she asked "Wouldn't it have been easier for you, dear, to sell everything on the spot instead of carting it all the way back here?"

"Fair go! This is the old man's stuff, all his bits and pieces, Mum."

"And the timber out in the garage, that was his too?"

"Sure. It'll come in handy for doing this place up one of these days. Knock out that kitchen window and put in one of his."

Mrs Ryan's legs began to tremble. She had to sit down on Vera's bed, scrunched up against the table legs. "This furniture — couldn't you store some of it at your place? You've got space now that the children have left home, haven't you?"

"Craig and Neville have left home, Mum. Sheryl is still with us."

"We like to keep the boys' rooms as they are in case they drop in for a night or two," Elsie explained.

There was something peculiar about this argument Mrs Ryan thought, but she couldn't put her finger on it. Harold shrugged at her, smiling, and went out of the room carrying a hatstand. Recognising the hatstand, Mrs Ryan burst out "How can Harold have any feeling for something that belonged to *him?*"

"You don't feel even the tiniest . . . anything now that he's dead?" Elsie asked.

Mrs Ryan's shoulders prickled again. "No. Why should I? He was a brute, Elsie. I couldn't start to tell you the things he did to us, me and Vera and Harold. I never have and I never will." What could you feel for someone who would torment a baby? That's what finally made up her mind to walk out on him. Bolt, more like it! "I think he was worse with Harold because it was a boy baby. He had to be cock of the walk."

"Harold got on well enough with him."

"Harold was a grown man by then. He was hardly likely to try anything on with a grown man, was he? Especially someone as big as himself."

"All I meant was . . . For years Harold believed his father was dead, Mum. I mean, Ryan isn't even his real name, is it? It's what *you* chose."

"That was for the best," Mrs Ryan said stubbornly. "Whatever I did, I did for the best."

Then for the next few minutes Mrs Ryan was too busy to mull over past history because Harold called Elsie and between them they carried the rest of the furniture into the house. "Not in the dining room, Harold!" cried Mrs Ryan (but it went in anyway). "Not the sitting room, you can't put a dressing-table in a sitting room, Harold! . . . I remember this dressing-table," she said after a moment. Now that he really was dead, why shouldn't they hear something? Slowly she rubbed one corner of the dressing-table with her apron. That was where I split my cheek

open, she thought. When he hit me that morning I fell
against the dressing-table and when he saw the blood he
shouted Why do you do it Mary, why do you make me so
angry I end up belting you, it isn't fair to a man!

"I remember this dressing-table, Harold," she began.

"Do you, Mum?" Harold's face lighted up. "I reckon
you're right. About a dressing-table in the sitting room, I
mean. We'll put it in your room."

In her chest a fist of pain hit her once, twice. "*No*,
Harold! Not there! Not in my room, Harold!"

She saw Elsie put her hand on Harold's arm. "What
about your room?"

Picking up Mr Magoo, Mrs Ryan followed them as they
staggered along the passage into Harold's room. From
each room of the house except her own, something of her
husband's looked back at her with blank mocking eyes.

In Harold's room she searched about for the little nip,
the scallywag. "Son," she began. Trembling, she made her
breath sidle past that knotted fist. "Harry! Not in here
either! You and Elsie can take that dressing-table right
back to Vera's room. Well, *make* space, Harold. Because
I'm taking in a boarder —" A boarder? The idea flowered
wildly. "I'm taking in a boarder and he'll want your room
and he won't want it choked up with *his* things."

"A *boarder?*" cried Harold and Elsie.

"Someone to keep an eye on me, check I haven't broken
my heart, a nice young man in Harry's room who'll put a
new washer in the tap and prune the fruit trees and bring
me a bunch of flowers now and then." She saw Harold
glance at Elsie: the old girl's off her twat. "I just hope for
your sake Harold he doesn't have a motor car because if he
does you and Elsie will just have to cart all that junk in the
garage right out again, won't you?"

"You've already got someone?" breathed Harold.

"Mum, how on earth will you manage?" asked Elsie with

silky concern. "All the extra work, Mum."

"He'll see to that — cook for himself, put out the washing —"

"But men are so helpless about these things," Elsie insisted.

"A young lady then," Mrs Ryan said faintly.

"I thought you said you already had some bloke," Harold said, taking a step towards the dressing-table.

At that very moment Mr Magoo jumped down out of Mrs Ryan's arms and Harold trod on him. Mr Magoo shrieked, spat. Bell jangling, he flew out of the room.

"Bloody cat!" shouted Harold.

"*Harold!*" said Mrs Ryan, in what Vera used to call her *watch out* voice.

Harold and Elsie glanced at each other, shrugged. Picking up the dressing-table, they took a few more chips of brown paint off the doorway as they set off once again towards Vera's room.

Mrs Ryan hurried out to look for Mr Magoo. She found him crouched near the garage, fluffed up to twice his size. "Poor little man," she muttered, stooping. At once that blackness threatened her. She had to fight it, breathing hard as she stood up, the cat in her arms. "It's all right, lovie. That brute'll soon be gone. And then soon as we've had a bit of a rest me and you'll get along to the corner shop and stick a notice in the window: URGENT, ROOM TO LET. Eh Mr Magoo? It's for the best, I reckon."

STUDENTS

"The contention is valid, of course," Jonathan is saying. He's still talking about some lecture.

"On the other hand —" He leans forward eagerly, jarring the small table they are sitting around. "Shift the perspective a bit —" He glances from face to face, trying to catch Sally's eye across the bowl of sweet peas she has filched from somebody's garden.

"Prisoners of our own discourse, you mean?" says Jenny in her breathless way, leaning across Paul.

"Death of the author," says Jonathan, and laughs. "Lord keep me wicked till I die!" he sings, sloshing port into his glass. He glances at Sally again. Laugh, pleads his look. She scrapes back her chair. "Why don't you just drop dead!" she says, and plunges out of the room.

Around the table no one's eyes meet. Jonathan hears her footsteps falter to a walk as she climbs the outside staircase. Usually she bounds up two steps at a time. The upstairs door slams. He looks away as the sweet peas shudder in the centre of the table. Then the others, two guys dropped in after the lecture, and Jenny and Paul from the group in the house to which this backyard flat belongs, go on talking as though nothing has happened. Paul refills glasses. Jenny, leaning towards Jonathan again, takes up his comment as though it's the most original thing she has heard. She expands it with a point of her own. "Wouldn't you say, Jonathan?"

He flinches from the pity in her eyes. As soon as he can without appearing to run after Sally he extricates himself from the discussion and goes out and upstairs. On the landing he pauses, looking across the slate roofs and chimney pots and treetops to the solid brick buildings of the university. An ambulance siren screaming towards the big hospital nearby jars him; turning the door knob quietly he goes into their bedroom. Her clothes pulled inside out lie scattered across the floor. It is still daylight but she has gone to bed, like a little girl in disgrace, he thinks, smiling. Since they've been together he has often been out to her parents' home, where there are three younger children, four now with the baby, and images of family life come easily to mind.

"Sally?"

Her head turns his way but her gaze goes right through him.

Perplexed, he sits on the edge of the bed. Her breath catches. He stares at the posters. Einstein in a leather jacket (his). Virginia Woolf (hers). "All Property is Theft!" (hers). At last, as he is wondering whether to risk speaking first or simply get up and go out again, she sighs. "I'm sorry. I'm sorry, Jonathan."

"It doesn't matter," he says gratefully. "Come downstairs again . . . Come for a walk, then."

She shakes her head, says all she wants to do is go to sleep.

"Now? Before dinner?"

"I don't want any dinner."

As he leans down to her the freckles in her white face stand out then run together. "Let me love you first. You'll sleep better. You always do." He smiles at her. Waits for an answering smile. Waits.

Even now, after all these months, he can't quite believe that it's true. That the Jonathan before Sally is no more than a fiction . . . *poor old Arthur's boy poor kid always stuck in some book . . . smile kid it might never happen* . . . He puts the beginning of his real self, his imagined self, at a moment in the queue on enrolment day. At first as he looked around, hating the other freshers all jabbering at one another, no one else gauche enough to come dressed in their speech night gear, he felt like catching the first train back to the country. What did he think he'd find here that was any different? As he weighed up his father's disapproval against his pleasure at having company again, the girl standing in front of him turned and asked him something. *Sally*. His stupid memory always lets him down over those first words. Something about the subjects being offered. But he does recall the exact tone of her voice: genuine, his father would call it. Not like the girls back home, girls at parties or in milk bars beckoning like Macbeth's witches and every one of them failing his GBS test. "Lord keep me wicked till I die!" he would slip in at the first opportunity, humming it a bit perhaps, waiting for her face to brighten with recognition: GBS! "Blanco Posnet," he would add by way of footnote. They thought he meant some new rock group. It flashed upon him as she spoke that he should try old Blanco again. "? ? ? ? ?" she asked. She was wearing jeans with zips everywhere and an orange and purple tee shirt with a pink ♀ embroidered on the pocket (that stick figure cut off at the pelvis he calls it, just to stir her). She was very tan. He became so conscious of his own pallor from spending the summer with Hardy and Lawrence and Shaw in his father's library that all he could reply was "What? What's that?" She repeated the question. She must have been satisfied with whatever he said then because she went on talking. She wasn't sure about this place, she said. Whether she could handle it, she meant. "I'm the first person in my family ever to go to university," she told him. He glanced again at the symbol on her shirt. "Well, it's good that the first one is a woman," he replied, hoping the comment would please her.

"Yes, but what's it all for?" she asked. (She often comes out with things like that: not seriously, he tells himself, more to stir him and Jenny and Paul). She said "Sometimes I think I should have stuck to my job instead of this big wank —" and she flicked the pages of her hand-book. "But what about knowledge! What about truth!" he shot back at her. He recalled a phrase he'd come across skimming in the library. "What about what Mary Wollstonecraft has to say about the intellect governing?" (He felt rather pleased with that.) "You can get that gardening," she told him. Her last job was gardening. She'd been working for two years so that she'd be eligible for Austudy. She couldn't afford university without Austudy. In the face of such initiative, experience, in-dependence, Jonathan felt a prickle of shame that all his expenses were being paid by his father. "He was set on me living in his old college," he explained. "He'd have liked me to do law like him, too, but at least I've made him happy about giving in over the college." (Jonathan always makes a mental apology to his father at this point: over the col-lege there'd been no *giving in*. Where else then could he see himself living? With his mother? On his own?)

The girl said "With all those grammar school yobs, huh? Think you'll like it?"

Her voice carried. The guy in front of her turned around. Unaware, she waited for Jonathan's reply. Their conversation was like a room with only themselves in it. "I'll probably just hide in my room with my nose in my books," he told her, and laughed. "That's what everyone at home thinks, anyway. Everyone from my town, I mean. There's just Dad and me at *home*. Maybe they're in for a big surprise!" he said with a swagger.

The girl looked at him. "There's loads of us," she said. "I'm the eldest. The youngest kid's just started school. Now my mother's got more time to do things I tried to get her to come here with me. As a mature age student. Lots of people your age start again, I told her. I said Mum, you could do whatever you want. She's so clever, you know? And guess what's happened? She's having another baby. She must be mad. No sooner is the last of the kids off her hands than she gets herself pregnant again."

Jonathan felt easy enough to try one of his jokes. "I suppose your father had something to do with it," he said, but the girl didn't notice.

"All the things she could be doing," she lamented, "And she gets herself pregnant!"

Did they really say all that waiting their turn to enrol? As the queue inched forward the girl exclaimed "I'm dying of thirst in here, aren't you?" "Let's get some iced coffee after this, shall we?" he suggested. "Ace!" said the girl. He didn't even know her name. And decided to skip Blanco Posnet. Just in case.

That night on impulse he phoned his mother from his college. His little sister answered. "Hi Jon! I'll get Mum." She never said more than that. He tried as he always did to reconcile this sister with the one from his childhood: the baby squealing with laughter in the racing pusher or throwing Rabbit out for him to pick up . . . burying her soft face in his neck . . . pressed rigid against her cot bars until, sick with terror himself, he would rush her out of the furious house — "*Jon*athan!" his mother exclaimed. "I've met some ace people," he told her. He could hear a man's voice in the background, and wondered who. "Thank God!" his mother replied. "Don't forget to tell your father," she added, meaning (Jonathan knew) See, I was right, all the boy needs is a bit more stimulus than he's getting in those backwoods. "Drop by sometime," she remembered to say before she hung up.

"Dear Dad, study's going well," Jonathan wrote in large writing on a postcard, hoping his father would assume from the brevity of the communication that he was far too busy with essays and things to write more. It was the afternoon he and Sally first went to bed together, on his lumpy bed in college. "Why not?" she said. "If we want to." He wanted her so much he was thinking of jumping off the college clock tower, he said. Sally laughed. "A little bit of blackmail, huh?" It was her first time too, she told him. Well, almost. If you counted how you felt about someone, it was. There'd been a boy, oh *years* ago, that she'd thought she was in love with, she was crazy about him for a whole week and then as soon as it happened she couldn't stand a bar of him, and there was her boyfriend last year (since Jonathan insisted). He was a gardener too — that's how they met. He said digging deep made you think deep. Why do you want to go to university? he kept asking her. What's wrong with gardening? *Nothing*, she tried to tell him. Gardening's fine, she just felt like a change. Why? he kept at her. Why, why, why? In the end she gave him the shove — she laughed at her own joke — not the shovel, the shove.

Then she said "But you're different, Jonathan, you respect me."

"I love you," he said. And was astonished at how simple it was, after all.

*   *   *

"Do you?" she said. "Do you really? I wish we could move out together somewhere. Into a group house or something. I'm fed up with living at home."

He wished he had thought of that. It seemed such a natural thing to do next the top of his head throbbed as he imagined all the things that could go wrong. "What would your parents say?" he asked, thinking how disappointed his father would be if he moved out of college. "Wouldn't you miss going home to your family?"

Sally laughed. "Come out to our crazy house sometime and see for yourself."

It was his first real invitation anywhere since he left home. "Sally!" he said. "I love you. Sally, Sally!"

"Sally. Let me. You'll sleep better." Drawing down the doona he puts his face to her breasts, taking one nipple then the other in his lips, sucking, caressing them with his tongue until they grow taut. She pulls away.

"Don't!"

"They won't hear, they're too busy talking . . . When, then? When?" Whispering. Urgent. Mock-petulant. "Let me, you wouldn't this morning."

She says coldly they can't screw for at least two weeks, she's just had an abortion.

Her freckles swim back into focus.

"You didn't tell me."

She says nothing, just draws the doona up to her chin and stares at him. "You didn't tell me," he repeats, and then, for something to clutch at, "When was it?"

"This morning."

"This morning? Today?"

She sighs. "Look, I wasn't at the library today, I skipped those lectures because I had an appointment at the abortion clinic and then I came home and spent the rest of the day in bed." With one foot she pushes a hot water bottle out on to the floor. "I don't need that, the cramps have stopped now."

"*Sally!* You had to go through all that by yourself — by yourself!" He tries to follow her to the clinic . . . the anonymous masked doctors, the lights sharp as scalpels and then the bright blood pulsing.

"Jenny waited at the clinic. The whole thing only took a couple of hours. I feel fine now, really I do. I'll be back at lectures tomorrow."

"Jenny? You told *Jenny!*" He recalls the pitying looks around the table just now. "And Jenny told Paul, I suppose." Downstairs someone opens the door and goes across the yard to the lavatory. "I wish you felt like getting dressed so we could go somewhere else and talk."

"What for?"

"What for? Well, because I had a part in it. I was responsible, too." He smiles at her, trying to think what it might mean, pregnant, child, but can get no further than images of their lovemaking, her hands on him, cradling, and her secret grainy lips.

She props herself up on one elbow. "You know what I told the counsellor? I said I didn't know who the father was. There *was* no father."

The walls of the room threaten to move out, dissolve. "But I was — I was —"

She sighs again. "Of course you were. Why do you always jump to conclusions?"

"Then why — I don't understand. Since it was mine." The word tastes strange, and he repeats it. "Mine, Sally."

"Mine, mine," she mocks.

"My child as well as yours," he hears himself persist.

"Well it's too late now, Jonathan."

"Yes of course. I'm sorry. I'm saying the first thing that comes into my head."

"What you're really saying is, I should have kept it, aren't you?" she suddenly shouts, and he winces, frowning at her, begging her to lower her voice. "I knew you would, I just knew it! Like my mother with all those kids at her heels and her too whacked for anything more intellectual than *Country Practice* — that's how you see women, isn't it?"

He opens his mouth to say she knows very well he never generalises, there are academics who lecture on *Country Practice*, and anyway one child isn't five. What he actually says is "Your mother is one of the nicest people I know! Every time she sees me she asks how I'm getting on, if I'm being fed properly, eating properly I mean —"

She isn't listening. "Remember when I went home a couple of months ago to help Mum with the baby when she was just out of hospital?"

He nods. Living here on his own for those few weeks was horrible. Eerie. He was haunted by echoes, he jumped at the click of a lock.

"And you came out to stay one weekend. Remember?"

"Yes." He was crazy for her. Desperate. Soon after he arrived she said "Did you bring your washing, Jon? I'll show you how to run the machine." Her father cut in. "You see to it, girl! Let the man have his beer." Load the clothes evenly, she told him, measure the soap powder — Then abruptly turning, unzipping her jeans, she pulled his hand on to herself. Once as a child he had been taken wading in a blood-warm tidal pool. Kicking the laundry door half-shut, tearing at his own zip, he pushed her back against the washing machine and plunged into her. If she'd objected, said What if one of the kids! or Go easy, Jon, wait! he wouldn't have listened.

"— every time you looked at his big round face, Jon, and his funny bald head with that spot pulsing and those enormous ears, one of them stuck out sideways and the other crumpled over like a new little cabbage leaf, and his little transparent fingers that grabbed on to mine —"

The washing machine changed cycles. Its vibration through her body drove him into a brief frenzy. Laughing breathlessly, she slid down to the floor. Afterwards he thought, How could we? He never referred to it again, never made it one of their jokes, *Remember that time we?*

She is almost crying. "You fool! Did you ever stop to wonder how you'd get on lumbered with a kid of your own in this place because you'd have to do your share too you know, all the jumping up at all hours and the shitty nappies and we're not even halfway through our degrees yet and how would we *live* for God's sake? On my unmarried mother's pension and your handouts from your father? And what would *he* have to say? You know he can't stand me!" She pauses, watching him. He says nothing. Her voice rises. "He thinks I'm no good for you — some scheming female — buggering up the future —"

"Stop it!" he hisses, trying not to shout himself. "Whenever has my father said anything like that?"

"Never *said* it."

"Anyway, isn't what you're saying all rather beside the point?" he asks, forcing himself to think calmly. "I haven't said one word to you about keeping it, not one word, only wondered why you didn't tell me — told other people but not me — though if you *had* wanted to keep it —" He looks around the room with its bed and dressing-table and small mirrorless wardrobe as though he's placing a baby's things somewhere.

"I could have got a job for a while," he muses. "In Dad's office, maybe. We've both talked about taking a year off sometime."

"To travel! To travel, Jon!"

"Well why not? Three of us instead of two — if that's what you'd wanted."

"That really is the *pits*."

"People do, Sally. I see them at the market sometimes, with those little papoose things."

"Will you shut up! Will you just shut up! It's *done* now, Jonathan. All I want to do is go to sleep and forget."

"I'm sorry. Of course you do. You have a really good sleep." He stands up. "Is there anything you want, darling?"

"No."

"I'll go down to the others, then." At the door he hesitates. "When do you think it happened, getting pregnant I mean?"

She sighs. "About eight weeks ago. I forgot to take the pill."

His hand drops from the door knob. "You mean . . . you haven't been using anything — and *I* haven't — Oh *why* didn't you tell me?"

She shrugs. "It was only the once. I took two the next day to make up."

He stares at her in bewilderment. "But the risk!"

She shrugs again. "Look it was bad luck, but it happened, so I had to do something, all right? Like getting a splinter and having to pull it out. Yes, it was no different from pulling out a splinter. Just a bit of discomfort and then — phhht! — gone."

. . . *given the shove/the shovel/the shove*. He opens the door. "You scare me, Sally." As she turns her face to the wall he is slashed by memories of raised voices and slammed doors, cases flung into taxis, Rabbit lying somewhere unwanted. Before he can stop himself he cries out, his voice breaking with self-pity, "That little kid! You never gave a damn, did you!"

* * *

The room shudders as he hurries down the staircase. Turning her head, Sally stares through the small curtainless window at the greying sky. A gust of laughter sweeps up from downstairs. Voices grow warm in debate . . . She listens eagerly but can't make out the words. Slowly, slowly, she runs her hands over her stomach. Tears harsh as blood ooze into her pillow.

TOURIST

But which shower to choose? There are two on your floor of the *pensione*, each curtainless, one so small and steamy that you have to leave the door ajar and risk a stranger bursting in — a stranger, probably, who will squawk at you in Italian — the other so eccentric that water sprays all over the walls and your nearly-new dressing gown and trickles into the passage. Which shower shall I try today? you would like to ask someone. Which shower shall I try today? you say in your head, jokey, so that whoever is listening can have no inkling of the small panic that underlies the silly question. Perhaps, after all, you should have played safe and booked into a hotel? But, as you put it to them back home in the tearoom during one of those sessions when you examined your plans from every angle (hogging the tea-break probably but that is a traveller's privilege) of course I can afford a hotel, you said, but a *pensione* in Rome sounds more *fun*. Well of course a *pensione* is more fun! came their prompt reply. More fun. More real. Let your hair down properly while you're about it — and you saw them exchange smiles. Be a devil! Take the plunge! Where's your sense of adventure?

So, when you are showered and dressed in your sensible dark blue, that gold ring from your Christmas bon-bon slipped on to your wedding finger, your handbag slung travelwise over one shoulder and your camera over the other, all ready to plunge, you ask yourself what to look at today. They were full of advice, of course. The Forum. The fountains. The churches. Yesterday, because it was close to your *pensione*, you looked through an ancient basilica with a magnificent ceiling of plundered gold. To-day you have a craving to be outdoors, to throw yourself into the Roman throng. The Via Veneto is a must, they told you. (They pronounced it Ven*ee*to, and so do you.) That's where the Beautiful People hang out, they said. You sit at a sidewalk cafe on the Via Ven*ee*to and you drink a leisurely cup of coffee and you watch the passing parade, imagine! an Italian film star straight off the set, or a fashion designer, or an oil baron jetted in from the Gulf. If you don't see the Beautiful People you haven't seen Rome, they smiled. You look up "Rome at Night" in your guide book and it is just as they said. It sounds so simple you almost believe it possible. "On the Via Veneto spend a few evening hours simply sitting," says the guide book. "You'll be glad you did." The Beautiful People beckon; they brush you with elegant eyelashes. You swan downstairs from the floor with the idiosyncratic showers and in the chair in the tiny reception room you practise sitting.

The manager, a young man less good-looking than your preconceived notions, is speaking on the telephone in rapid Italian. When he has finished he switches to English as easily as he clicks down the receiver. "Good morning, Signora. Can I help you at all?" Thank you. I am just put-ting my courage together — "I'm just checking my map" is what you actually say, unfolding the map and turning it this way and that. "Let me know if you need any help, Signora," he repeats, turning his attention to a young cou-ple who have just arrived. Dropping rucksacks almost on to your feet, they begin *"Guten Morgen —"* then laugh tiredly and try in Italian. *"Guten Morgen. Ich spreche*

deutsch," he says gently. An English-speaking guest you
exchanged nods with at breakfast asks if there's anywhere
close by to get a good, cheap lunch, dinner as well maybe.
"Turn right and right again and you'll find an excellent
locanda," says the manager, adding "Tell Roberto that
Giovanni sent you." The guest hurries out, the Germans
make their way upstairs, the manager busies himself with
his books. You warm towards this Giovanni, so helpful, so
reassuring, and you search your mind for some request of
your own. On your map you can locate the Trevi Fountain
(the most romantic in Rome, they swooned, teasing you
about what to wish), but the Via Veneto isn't so easy. You
are about to ask him to point it out when he suddenly looks
up. "Signora, your bag and your camera over your
shoulder like that — *not* a good idea. In Rome unfor-
tunately at this time of year we have many *scippatori*,
young men on motorpeds on the lookout for women such
as yourself, a tourist, that is, with valuable articles on
straps which they seize as they ride by." He leans towards
you, his eyes like boiling black coffee. "And if you imagine
to hang on you will be dragged along the pavement and
your knees smashed!" What are you to do? As you stare at
him in perplexity he adds "Only a suggestion, of course,
but can you not carry what you need in a body belt? Then
you are not quite such an obvious target." Oh but you hate
a body belt! It is so awkward and clumsy — so sweaty —
unfeminine. How could he be so insensitive! You slump in
your chair.

Somehow, finally, your camera gets locked away in the
pensione safe, someone whom in your fluster you forget to
thank holds the lobby door open for you, and you pass out
into the street, your shoulder bag clamped to your stomach
and your ears attuned to the put-put of the *scippatori*.
Everyone rides a motorped, it seems, even a priest with flat
black hat and swinging crucifix. In the streets is a babble of

tongues. And you are part of it all! How you wish someone could take your photo to send them as proof. You keep away from the Metro, of course, because of the gipsies — those women, they warned you, their eyes lighting up at your consternation, those great dark women on the Metro stairways who will crowd you into a corner, thrust a plate of *cassata* into your face, and rob your pockets. Murmuring those phrases in capitals in the Berlitz guide: STOP! *AIUTO! POLIZIA!* and stepping carefully because of all the dog dirt, and the rank streams fanning out from the corners of buildings, you turn in the general direction of the Trevi Fountain.

In a small square you come unexpectedly upon the Fountain of Tortoises, four graceful naked youths each supporting a tortoise that is scrambling to drink at the upper basin. As you watch, one of them flips his tortoise right into the pool and, hopping down from his shell-shaped perch, says Come Signora, together you and I will see Rome. Upon which the second jumps down: Come with me, Signora . . . then the third, and the fourth. What are you to do? Which one to choose? You twist and twist the gold bon-bon ring, trying to decide, and when they catch sight of it as it glints in the sun, each murmurs *Mi dispiace, Signora*, and leaps back on to the fountain. The water flows, the tortoises clamber, you walk on alone.

As for the Trevi — you feel a shock of disappointment. It is so grandioise, the water so sluggish and green, the marble youths twisting the necks of the seahorses so cruel. In the great pool at the foot of the fountain real youths, loud and suntanned, paddle and kick and grimace at cameras. Coins glitter. You shoo away a pigeon and sit down, feeling rather silly at having to push through all the families and the couples just to toss away a good coin. In a dry grotto to one side of the fountain a man lies asleep, the full strength of the late summer sun beating down on his face. You sit for a long time, wondering what *they* would have you wish, and still he sleeps on.

At last, deliberately not wishing, your heart beating because you have in a sense defied *them*, you turn back towards the centre of the city. There, somewhere, the Beautiful People are beginning to stir. You wonder about that red-faced sleeper — should you have wakened him? Although it is early September, autumn already, Rome surprises you with its heat. Soon, striding along the Via del Corso, the Via Quattro Novembre, the Via Nazionale, you feel as embarrassed as a schoolgirl as great dark patches spread under the arms of your dress. You would like to throw it away. Buy yourself something new! they groaned. Get a new image! they shrieked. But when you venture into one of the dozens of little shops with the dazzling window displays, all your carefully rehearsed Berlitz phrases desert you; at the assistant's courteous *"Posso aiutarla?"* you do not look up, you go on fingering the garments, you actually pretend to be deaf. The ease of this out-of-character dissembling so shocks you that you hurry away in search of some quiet place to collect yourself. You walk swiftly past several fountains, along a steep street and into the very bowels of a large dark church. And it is not a church at all, you discover, but a charnel-house.

An old, old man in the brown robe of a religious order welcomes you towards a gallery. Here, arresting as any fashion window, are grottoes of human bones, centuries of bones, skulls, ribs, pelvises, layers of arm bones, layers of leg bones, all painstakingly selected for length and shape and worked into exquisite designs. Electric light filters through a crisscrossing of fingers. An arrangement of pelvises clasped within a rectangle of arm bones suggests a motto that you puzzle to decipher. A hooded skeleton in brown dusty garb grins at you over folded hands, inviting you to admire his artistry. From the wrinkled monk at the desk you buy a postcard picturing the soaring rose-patterned ceiling fashioned from vertebrae and thin, delicate ribs, and learn that you are in the *Cimetero dei Cappuccini*, the Capuchin Cemetery.

Outside, shivering a little although the sun is still power-ful, you hurry into the first bar you come to and, thrusting thousands of *lire* at the cashier, order *un cappuccino*. "*Un cappuccino*," you repeat, and begin to laugh, remembering those old dusty men amongst the bones, *i cappuccini* — a woman laughing alone in a public place in a foreign coun-try.

"Just a touch of the sun," you say to the person standing next to you at the counter, a woman carrying an English-language guide book. The woman smiles. You like her face; she has good bones. She is about your age, a bit younger, five or ten years maybe. "I've been out walking," you explain. She too looks as though she has been walking; she is wearing blue and white running shoes with pink laces. "There's more bite in the sun than you think," you continue, feeling terribly glad that you've met: two fellow travellers, sisters almost. "For this time of year," you add, noting with surprise that she doesn't bother with a protec-tive ring on her finger. Unobtrusively you slip yours off and drop it into your half-empty cup.

"That's true," says the woman.

She finishes her coffee. Hastily you say "I've been walk-ing since daybreak and still there's so much to see!"

"There certainly is," she agrees, pushing her cup across the counter.

"What have you seen today?" you demand before she can move away.

"Well!" She widens her eyes, remembering. "I started with the Forum —"

"And the churches!" you take up. "Have you seen the gold ceiling of Santa Maria Maggiore? No? Well, the Trevi

Fountain, then? *Everyone* goes there! What about the Capuchin Cemetery — you haven't seen the Capuchin Cemetery? Why, you haven't seen anything!"

Into the little silence that follows this, you pour a wonderful idea that has been frothing up in your mind since you got rid of that ring. "Listen, I know just the place to go at this time of day. The Via Veneto. You know about the Via Veneto? It's where people go with their friends to drink and eat dinner and then sit over coffee to watch the Beautiful People go by, the Aga Khan's grandson, Gucci, Sophia Loren, all that crowd. It's not expensive," you add, glancing at her running shoes. "All the tourists go there — all my friends — if you don't see the Via Veneto you haven't seen Rome!"

"Well!" she says again. "It does sound rather fun, doesn't it? Where is it?"

"Oh it's quite nearby." But when you spread out your map, and she spreads out hers, you can find the Via Veneto neither listed in the index nor on the map itself. "*Scusi, Signor,*" you read carefully from your phrase book to the Italian standing on the other side of you. "*Dove Via Veneeto? Si Signor, Via Veneeto!* . . . Never mind," you say to your new friend. "I'm sure it's this way." In the Via Quattro Fontane you accost a young man, "*La Via Veneeto*, please, *per piacere?*" but he shrugs and walks on. At the Piazza della Repubblica — where you are only a few minutes' walk from the Metro and your *pensione*, you realise — your friend says "Well, these Beautiful People seem pretty elusive, don't they, and I'm just about whacked."

"Of course, because you need to eat," you encourage her. "I know the very place, just a few steps from here. And Roberto will know all about it. And then we can go there together, you and I, for coffee."

But the woman shakes her head. "Some other time,

maybe. But *you* go, the Via Veneto sounds fun."

"Well of course it's fun!" you snap. "But I can hardly go alone, can I?"

"Why not?" says the woman. *Why not?* How stupid this woman has become! You part then, and when you have had a second shower at the *pensione* (in the other one this time) and changed your dress and taken a headache powder, you turn right and right again and find Giovanni's *locanda*. It is, as you anticipate, a very ordinary place, clean, but with nothing notable about its lighting or ceiling or anything, an anonymous place. A waiter whom you assume is Roberto motions you to a table on the pavement with a grace that reminds you of the youths with the tortoises — except that he wears clothes, of course, and has a petulant mouth. He is so slow in bringing the menu that you decide to keep quiet about Giovanni's commendation. His manner becomes positively disdainful when you order the only familiar dish on the menu, *spaghetti bolognese*, instead of being adventurous and starting off with *soppressata* as he suggests. When he is not taking orders he is hanging around a table where a young woman is sitting alone. She has an American accent, and you overhear Roberto saying "I lika to practise, the Eenglish, when, the occasion, presents." The *locanda* becomes busy, the young woman is joined by a young man, and Roberto moves away. At the table on the other side of you sit two girls, sixteen or eighteen perhaps, who do not eat but drink cup after cup of *caffè espresso*. The young woman talks earnestly in Italian to the young man, telling him her life story, you decide, telling him about the husband who isn't with her, the boss who won't promote her, her wedding ring flashing as the words pour. She has all his attention. An enormous motorbike roars past, turns, and stops opposite the table with the two girls. Roberto appears at the doorway and stands transfixed. At last he looks down at you, his eyes warm now, responsive, and murmurs "Is magnificent bike, is Ducati, can do more than two hundred twenty!" The motorcyclist, leaning back with his feet propped on the ground, calls out. The girls exchange glances, then the one with her back to the street lights a cigarette, inhales and blows a smoke ring over her head. The motorcyclist waits. The young man on the other side of you is now holding the American woman's hand. The second of the two girls beckons Roberto and orders more coffee. Still the motorcyclist waits. And then the girl with her back to him jumps up, runs across to him, speaks, he guns the engine and is gone. The noise of it, even as it grows fainter, pierces the ordinary traffic. The two girls stare at each other. At the first table the woman has retreated, the man is leaning towards her, she is shaking her head. And then you hear the familiar throb of that motorbike. The girls jump up as it circles, both of them climb on to the pillion seat and away they blast. The American woman has dropped her head, her body quiescent now, it is he who is talking, talking, still she shakes her head but now both hands are holding hers, his fingertips move along her arms.

The *locanda* has become crowded. A waiting couple fidgets near your table. Roberto makes it clear with an impatient swish of his serviette that he would like you to pay and go. Surely this day can not end so inconclusively? You make one last frantic effort. "*Scusi, Signora?* Perhaps if the *Signora* writes —" and he hands you a pencil stub. "Ah! *Si, Via Veneto, Signora! Via Vittorio Veneto.* You have the map, *Signora?*" And with a lofty smile he points to it at once, so obvious now, Via Vittorio Veneto (only your eye stopped at *Ve* in the index), Via Vittorio Veneto, the street of the Beautiful People, no more than a few minutes from where you actually were earlier, at the Capuchin Cemetery.

"*Molto grazie! Una tazza di caffè, per piacere,*" you say, deliberately using Italian so he can't practise his English. To drown your terrible disappointment you take out your souvenir postcard and using Roberto's pencil stub you write, very small so as to fit it all in: "Hello back there! How's this! I'm at this very moment sitting amongst the Beautiful People at THE place to be. Name? *I Cappuccini.* You should see my shocking pink laces. My friend Roberto speaks English German Italian, he's so easy to talk to, he must have got my whole life story just over the *soppressata*. His hobby's Ducatis and he looks like —" You make a wild guess. "— looks like Gucci." As Roberto hovers, anxious for that table, you continue "He's *so* persuasive, I'll have to stop — *Ciao!*"

STORM

It's the thunder that wakes Chrissie Jennaway. She hears
the sizzle of rain and thinks Now the garden will be saved,
my lovely day lilies and the scarlet rhus. Something, a deck
chair, crashes over on the patio. *Rupert!* she whispers, but
Rupert goes on breathing, *out* in, *out* in. Chrissie bunches
her pillow around her ears.

She wonders if the others are awake. Philip has always
hated thunder, should she slip in and see? *Chrissie, I'm not
a kid any more.* And her niece in the guest room, storms
wouldn't scare Alvie. What would scare Alvie? Alvie takes
after her mother.

In an instant of light the bedroom curtains press towards
her like a big-bellied woman. She sits up. The windows —
every bedroom window will be open to the rain! A second
flash lights up Rupert's sleeping face in a bluish-white
glare. His flesh dissolves, the bones cast pits of shadow.
There is another shock of thunder, closer this time. Properly awake now, she puts back the sheet and swings her
legs over the side of the bed, grunting as she straightens her
back. It is hot in the bedroom, airless; her thighs slither
and stick as she fumbles across the room. For several
moments she stands in front of the open window, drawing
the storm's freshness deep into her chest, and lifting her
nightdress to let the small hard seeds of rain hit her skin.

The window ledge is wet. Feeling on the low chair near-by she finds her pants, the last thing she takes off after pulling on her nightie. She mops the ledge with them, then creeps out to the landing to check the windows in the other bedrooms.

It is the summer school holidays. Philip spends vacations with his father, school terms with his mother. It's his last holiday before he starts university. He's supposed to be assisting Rupert, making deliveries, learning the business. He has his licence now, but Rupert says he's next to useless while Chrissie's niece is in the house. They're forever nicking off, Rupert grumbles. To the beach, to the pictures, God knows where.

But Rupert, you're only young once, Chrissie pleads. They're so much in love, she thinks, giving herself a little hug. I wish we'd met when we were that age, Rupert. It's lovely, those secret glances over breakfast that they think I don't notice, and yesterday the pair of them running hand-in-hand down the drive and Philip putting his hands on the top of the gate and vaulting right over. He's so happy, poor kid, Alvie's made all the difference, I just hope that mother of his has noticed.

Out of habit she knocks on Philip's door before opening it. "It's only me, dear, doing a rain check," she whispers, then sees in another blue flash that Philip's bed is empty, in fact hasn't been slept in at all. Her first thought is, he hasn't come upstairs yet. They've gone out to a film — for a midnight swim — they're in the TV room watching TV. From downstairs comes the breath-held silence of empty rooms. She pulls the window shut, then tiptoes past the bed again and closes the door.

Leaning against the landing wall she makes herself breathe deep and slow. Suddenly the family clock that used to prod her off to school, to work, to church booms up at her: ONE. TWO. THREE. She goes straight into the guest room. The venetian blind is rattling wildly. She prays that the lightning will hold off till she is out of the room again, but like some horrid tattletale there comes a flash just as she turns from the window. She sees two heads turned to each other, her niece's pretty hair that Alvie says she wants crew cut fanned over the pillow and her stepson's arm fallen across the girl's hip. Chrissie's stomach lurches. Her own sister's child — in her care! She stares at the two sleeping so peacefully, oblivious of the night's storm. So sweet, she thinks, tears pricking her eyelids, then realises as she hears one of them sigh and the bed creak slightly that what she is still looking at is that split-second glimpse etched on to her brain.

She hurries out of the room. Should she slam the door? She closes it quietly. Back in her own bed, she hears Rupert breathing in that heavy way that means he is about to start snoring. She jabs at his shoulder. "Whass'matter? Whass'matter?" "You're snoring, Rupert." He mumbles " . . . wasn't me," and turns over.

She twitches on to her back, staring into the blackness. What should she do? Go back and knock on Alvie's door until the girl comes stumbling out to the landing, fuzzy with sleep and love? *Alvie I hope you know right from wrong*. But perhaps it's happened only this once. Perhaps nothing has *happened*. Excuse me dear, your window — But the window is already shut. Chrissie has shut it. In Chrissie's mind Alvie stares at her aunt, goes on staring until, lying in her safe bed next to Rupert, Chrissie begins to feel quite transparent, all legs and no petticoat like poor Lady Di in that photo that time.

The rain eases off. Chrissie hears a distant rumble of thunder. Maybe she should go right back into that room and, letting Alvie sleep on, put her hand firmly on Philip's shoulder and say — say what? Go back to your own bed, son, and we'll say no more about it. Because he is her son, isn't he, the only child she'll ever have, even if she does have to share him with that undeserving woman?

But if she says that, if she says *Philip we'll say no more*, then he and she will have a secret against Philip's father — against Rupert, her own husband — just as once, when she was still Chrissie Lafferty, secretary, she and Rupert had a secret against Philip's mother, and, come to that, a secret against Philip himself since he used to come into the office sometimes to see his dad, and Chrissie would bend over her typewriter and pretend to be working very hard when really she was taking peeks at the little chap in school uniform and the too-big cap who always said "Good afternoon, Miss Lafferty" in that ducky old-fashioned way so that it was all she could do not to reach out and give him a hug —

Oh I wish it was morning! wails Chrissie. She's happiest under her old straw donkey's breakfast, tying up a sprawling pink, nipping out a weed, picking a bunch of roses for Rupert's desk at the office. Her head grows full of roses, the buds swelling, opening, their perfume so delicious she could snatch it to herself in heady gulps.

She forces herself awake again. Do nothing, then? She holds her breath, listening for the creak of bedroom doors. They looked so . . . sweet, she thinks again, turning to plant her feet against Rupert's thin shanks. Calf love, Rupert calls it. Puppy love. A pair of school kids. They'll get over it soon enough, he says. The girl goes back to the country in a couple of days Chrissie and in less than a month Philip will be mixing with a totally different crowd. Chrissie frowns. But they're so in love, Rupert. It's like Romeo and Juliet. Or those two children, the girl and the boy stranded on the island in *Blue Lagoon*.

Sharp as a cramp a memory surfaces. It's the school social. She's pretending she has to run out to the supper room to check on the hot water and the plates of limp sandwiches and butterfly cakes with slithery purple jelly —

anything rather than endure watching the other girls asked to dance, her head pressed back against the wall and a whalebone smile stretching her mouth.

Alvie's mother Joannie, the little minx, always had some boy hanging about, she was boy-mad, always sneaking off to meet someone, *Chrissie don't tell Mum, promise you won't tell Mum!* And yet Chrissie was the pretty one even if she does say it herself, skin like cream because it was before this craze for frying yourself to a chip, and thick fair hair she brushed two hundred strokes every night — awful how your hair thins out as you get older, she couldn't grow it long again if she tried, and here's young Alvie saying maybe she'll try shaving her head, I've never felt fresh air on my scalp says Alvie, it would be an experience, and Philip smiles, Philip just smiles.

Philip, Chrissie rehearses. Philip, you must promise me —

Promise what? To be good? But what is *good?* Her own life, for instance, herself and Rupert — Rupert was a married man with a child, but so unhappy, so dreadfully lonely, it's true what he told her, she was the only good thing in his life, really and truly the only good thing, though it took her a long time to understand that. She never intended to be *the other woman*, to come between husband and wife, to deceive people, her own family, the child.

The clock strikes four, or five was it? It will be morning soon, breakfast time. She sees the four of them sitting around the table, young Alvie and Philip exchanging sly looks, Rupert oblivious behind the morning paper, herself making toast, refilling cups, big with secret knowledge. *Oh* . . . moans Chrissie, pinching folds of her nightdress through her fingers, I don't want secrets, what can I do with secrets? Drawing her nightdress right up she clasps her plump stomach, smooths her fingers over the soft flesh and into moist stealthy creases. Now that the room has grown cooler, she becomes through her probing fingers a spring garden within whose chilly depths bulbs and seeds and roots are secretly moving, swelling out, growing heavy and mysterious then bursting open into a thousand throbbing flowers.

Inadvertently her foot scrapes Rupert's leg. He wakes up saying "What's the matter? Was I snoring?"

"No." Pulling the sheet under her chin, she turns away. Rupert tugs at his share of the sheet. She holds on to it.

"What's the matter with you, Chrissie? Can't you sleep, dear?"

"Oh Rupert!" She is nearly crying with the relief of having him there.

The bed jars as Rupert's feet find the floor. Chrissie hears the landing light click on, hears him shout

"PHILIP!"

Oh Rupert, wails Chrissie to herself, pulling the sheet over her face against the glare of the light. Oh why did that storm have to blow up? There'll be such a mess to sweep up in the garden!

A LOVE STORY

(I) Legend

When Philip wakes again it is daylight; as window, washbasin, chair and then rucksacks swim into focus, this time he knows where he is: in a room in a *pensione* in Florence, exams over, his girl beside him just a stone's throw from the bridge where Dante saw Beatrice. Three months of travelling. Seeing. Voyage to Discovery. New World finds Old. He turns his head; Alvie is still asleep. Sitting up carefully, he watches a pulse ticking in her neck. Her skin is pale, winter-pale, but across the pillow her hair is a copper fire. She has used the rinse she bought to try out her phrase book Italian. Her lips move; she is smiling. At what, he wonders, sliding out of the bed. What?

Shivering in the cool of late autumn, he pulls on jeans and skivvy and, lifting the chair over to the window, opens his notebook. What he reads there doesn't seem too bad, quite good in fact. Before she wakes up he will have another go at it, see if this morning he can't pin down in verse all the dazzle of paint, the curve and gleam of marble that has made him feel drunk — stoned — feverish since he stepped off the plane back in Rome.

He glances across at Alvie; her eyelids flutter. Stay asleep darling, he begs. Let me get this right first. Alvie is a bit terse sometimes about his notebook — a habit grown out of all that solitariness, a whole four-fifths of his life actually, so long he used to think being alone was fate's lot for him. She says it's an obsession, this need to get it right. Just dash off a few impressions she says, the rest will come later, you know it will. Stop *worrying*, Phil. Relax. Take a deep breath. Take more photos — they'll bring it all back. Or postcards — buy postcards like me. And she flicks through things that have caught her eye: a fountain in Rome that they came upon unexpectedly at the end of a long day when they were on the edge of quarrelling; and that statue of the naked boy about to kiss his girl; nice that, she says, Love hugging his Psyche.

What she doesn't understand, broods Philip, hunched up under the window, is that it's not simply a matter of making notes of everything like some indiscriminate camera. No. That isn't bothering him. It's the shape within all the shapes and colours — *that's* what keeps eluding him.

He looks down at his notes. It's no good, the words won't move, they lie shrivelled and limp. His head begins to thump. He feels chilled right through. Dropping the notebook he goes to his rucksack and drags out a thick winter shirt, then gives the rucksack a great shove across the floor.

Alvie mumbles; opens her eyes. "Up already?"

"It isn't exactly early."

"What's eating you?"

"I've got a headache."

"Bad? How bad?"

"It's like those snakes wound around old man Laocoön," he tells her, rather pleased with that, glancing across at her as he buttons his cuffs.

She laughs. "It's probably all that Chianti you've been drinking. You want to watch it, Phil." She yawns, stretches, pushes her hair off her face. Pulling a blanket around herself she comes across to the window. "Want me to rub your head?"

"Yes please." Head against her breast he tells her, "When I woke up in the middle of the night I couldn't remember where I was. It was horrible." It is the ghost of a childhood terror: waking to a darkness that gave him back nothing but his screams until alarmed, impatient, blinking as she switched on his light, his mother would rush in.

Alvie's fingertips on his temples move in slow firm circles. "You soon remembered," she says drily.

"You smell good," he murmurs, breathing in a mixture of sleepiness and yesterday's sweat and the ardour of his pre-dawn clinging.

She laughs again. "So do you. Maybe that's it — compatible whats-its-names." His hands take in the familiar sharpness of her hip bones, the smoothness of skin. Her thighs part slightly. She says "Where are we off to today, Phil — the Accademia, is it? What's so funny?"

"You. Saying that. Where are we off to today. Remember that first holiday you spent at my father's when we were kids and I was supposed to be showing you the sights of Melbourne?" Like wine there courses through him memories of that frantic two weeks; those old things he loved that he wanted to show her, and the first time she touched him (it was outside the museum), and the kisses and fondling that nearly sent him crazy until on the very last night of her visit she said yes to him (he cleaned his teeth first, he remembers), a scared kid discovering with her what other kids sniggered about and poets sang about and his parents wrecked up his childhood fighting about. And himself? She had whispered "Quick get something, anything, yes your singlet'll do" because she was bleeding, loving her he had made her bleed but she hadn't cared, she'd said "Don't be shocked, Philip, I'd rather it was you than anyone" and he had cried with the joy of her.

"I remember." The blanket slips from her shoulders as she waves her hand at their pile of guide books and mementoes. "So here we are. So what's new."

He looks at her, sees the delicacy of marble. An idea hits him. "That statue of Apollo pursuing Daphne in that gallery in Rome — you know, the one by Bernini —" They had walked around it for ages, marvelling at the desperation the sculptor had caught, the cry for help, the youthful arms outstretched, the swirling cloak covering the lust doomed to marble imprisonment forever as the nymph's flesh at his touch turns to wood.

"The letch with the hots for the leafy lady — that one?"

It's the poet clutching at his muse, he thinks excitedly. Scooping up his notebook and scrawling "Bern's Ap →Daph = me → inspiration", he tells her "I know exactly how frustrated that poor bugger felt!"

For a moment she stares at him, then pulling on her tracksuit and snatching up towel and soap she retorts "Oh you do, do you? Just what *do* you think happened when you woke me up at four o'clock this morning?"

But whether she is offended or pretending he's not sure because when he starts to explain what he meant she shuts him up with one of her kisses, and when he grabs her towel to pull her on to the bed with him she turns it into a wrestling match which she wins by escaping into the passage.

(II) Odalisque

Breakfast in the *pensione* is served until nine.

It is now twenty past.

Philip, arranging his damp shirt on a hanger by the window, says "It's hardly worth going down, is it?" but Alvie, pulling a comb once through her wet hair, jangles the room key at him, saying "Come *on*, we're paying aren't we?"

On the stairs maids are bundling heaps of linen. "Permesso!" she calls, bounding past them. "Bon jerno! Kommy star? Permesso!" "*Bon giorno, bon giorno!*" he echoes, relishing her easy warmth with strangers but wincing at her accent. In the dining room doorway they pause. The room is almost empty, the other guests well on their way to the Uffizi or the Ponte Vecchio by now. A waitress glances at them then goes on shaking cloths and laying clean cutlery.

She nudges him. "Me dispee-archie," she mews plaintively, then drops her head to her folded hands in a parody of sleeping. "Troppo! Troppo!" She nudges him again triumphantly as the waitress, sighing, waves them to a table by the window. "Wow! Just look at that sunshine, will you!" she exclaims, pulling the lace curtain aside so that he sees a brightening in the grey sky. "We're dead lucky, aren't we?" She peers at him around a fold of the curtain, her eyes round. "What if someone . . . ?" They burst out laughing. Under the table her feet find his.

He glances around the room. Is the waitress grinning? Is that disgust crossing the faces of the middle-aged couple whose eye he catches? He looks down at his hands,

momentarily convinced that what he still feels in his fingertips, his joints, along all his senses, must be apparent to
everyone — his hurrying with her towel to the shower cubicle at the end of the corridor and finding the door ajar
because the lock doesn't catch and her saying "Oh it's *you*,
is it?" goggling her eyes at him around the plastic curtain
then catching his shirt sleeve and trying to pull him into the
shower recess with her, laughing at his protests as his clean
shirt gets soaked, and then the two of them together in the
shower fighting over the miserable trickle of hot water,
feet skidding on the mouldy floor, hip bones jostling, her
body slippery with soap, tasting of soap, opening to his
urgency as though it's five years not five hours since they
last made love, water spraying everywhere and should
someone barge in only the greasy plastic shower curtain
dividing love from indecency.

The waitress brings two rolls and two pastries to their
table. "Go on," Alvie says, biting into one of them. "Eat
up, they'll be giving us the shove in a minute."

"Coffee? Tea?" the waitress asks.

"Kaffay con lattay," she replies, indicating him. It's
something they agreed on before they left home: to use
their little bit of Italian wherever they could; they'd feel
part of the place then; it would be more fun. "*Si, un caffè
con latte,*" he repeats. "*Per favore.*" But while he struggles
to find the correct word, the correct way to hold his
mouth, she slams the phrase book shut and plunges on.
She points to herself. "Daisy dayro . . . daisy dayro tay
con lattay freddo. *Freddo!*" she emphasises. "I can't
stomach tea with hot milk," she tells him, and she pulls
another of her faces, looking to him to laugh with her —
but at what? At funny foreign customs? At herself for being so pigheaded over cold milk in the cup first? He isn't
sure. But laughs anyway, because looking at her he is
reminded of a plant his stepmother grows in a sunny

garden bed, a joyous plant all pinks and reds and golds
amongst the dark green leaves of its neighbours. It catches
him with a shock of gladness each time he passes it. Love-
lies-bleeding, his stepmother calls it. Philip prefers
amaranthus, a name he looked up in the dictionary once
because he liked the sound of it: *amaranth, an imaginary
unfading flower*. Watching Alvie now as she drowns a
spoonful of brown sugar then chews it, the sort of silly
thing you remember years later about people, he thinks excitedly love is like that plant, not imaginary meaning
unreal but *imagined, of the imagination* — five minutes
fucking somewhere, bedroom, bathroom, each moment
gone as it's happening but the joy of it lasting, shaped in
your mind the way all the canvas and stone we've been
looking at these last few days has been worked on, shaped:
a glimpse of the unimaginable.

"Maybe we should catch a bus," she is saying, leaning
over the table to look at his watch. Her own watch is probably on the floor somewhere upstairs, one of her careless,
carefree habits. "If we don't sit down for a cappuccino
maybe we can afford a bus?"

"Yes," he says, concentrating on the spoon he is turning
in his cup. He wants her again. When they go upstairs to
clean their teeth he will have her again. And there rises the
certainty that from all the notes, bits of verse, impressions
filling page after page of his notebook he will shape a
poem more erotic than anything he has yet tried, a poem as
voluptuous as worked marble, as sensual as Titian's Venus
yesterday, the glowing flesh turned in love to whoever
looked at her, as unfading as an imaginary flower.

(III) Madonna

"It'll be good," he tells her as they climb on to the crowded bus. "It'll be different." Alvie pulls him towards two seats about to be vacated. "It'll combine everything I've felt about all this — this —" And he gestures widely to indicate: *everything*. Words spin into his mind. He begins to juggle phrases. So absorbed is he, staring into the aisle at nothing, that it is Alvie who sees them first. "Look!" she says, nudging him. "That cap on that girl — isn't it great?"

He looks. Along the narrow medieval footpath, walking in the same direction as the slow-moving bus, come two girls wearing jeans and leather jackets, sisters perhaps, one about twelve who is talking, gesticulating, skipping around people in her way, the other older, taller, her fair hair falling to her shoulders from under her Mao cap, and her hands as calm as her still, grave face. Where have they come from? Perhaps they live in one of these ancient jutting houses. If it were not for their clothes, he thinks, looking from one to the other as they catch up with the bus, they might have stepped out of a fifteenth century painting. The bus crawls past, then stops altogether. Horns toot. Ahead he can see a policeman waving his arms. He looks back at the girls, and sees a youth carrying a satchel and a rolled-up tube of paper approach the older girl and speak. She stops. The Angel Gabriel at the Annunciation, he thinks. The Angel Gabriel unrolls his scroll of paper and displays it. He has long dark hair and a soft cap like an upturned plant pot — "like the cap we saw in that painting yesterday!" Philip exclaims. "That Lippi self-portrait, remember?" Painted by the artist-son of an artist-priest and the nun Lucretia . . . "His father, Fra Filippo Lippi, he used to hop out of his monastery at night and rage around Florence — along this street maybe, Alvie!" He cranes across her.

She breathes into his neck. "Some guy, that Filippo. Looking for inspiration, was he? . . . I got a postcard of his Madonna, Phil," she adds, sitting up. "You know, the one with the little angel peeking over his shoulder?"

"Did you? It's lovely, isn't it?" Lucretia was probably the model for that painting. Philip likes to think so, anyway. He sees the priest at his easel, splotches of paint on his black garb, capturing forever the girl he has smuggled into his cell. Look at the Christ-Child, he tells them. You must all look at the Christ-Child. Lucretia, dazed with his kisses, folds her quivering hands and lowers her eyes, but one of the little angels won't keep his head still. Smiling, he turns to see what the painter is doing . . .

It's Fra Filippo out there and he wants to paint her. The youth and the girl confer earnestly. As the youth takes more papers from his satchel the younger girl, the little sister, looks from one to the other with, well not a smirk exactly, smirk's a bit coarse —

At last the girl gives back the sheets of paper, reluctantly Philip thinks, and the youth rolls them up again. Fastening his satchel he goes on his way. Just then the bus lurches forward through a gap in the traffic, and Philip's last sight of them is of the little sister laughing outright, and the girl glancing over her shoulder at God's messenger, curious and secretly pleased —

"Dirty postcards, I bet," says his Madonna, shoving him in the ribs with her elbow.

(IV) The Slaves

Hunching their shoulders, they cross the piazza. It is weather for moving briskly, but two middle-aged women in black have stopped to chat under the bare trees, their hands in fingerless gloves, bread and vegetables clutched in their arms. Their laughter rings like metal. A few people, off-season tourists like Alvie and Philip perhaps, are gazing up at the facade of the great church, or poring over maps. Pigeons fly down to a child who is scattering a few crumbs. At the rapid approach of a black-robed priest, his heavy cross swinging, the pigeons fly up in a swoop of wings, then settle again hungrily. One white pigeon, however, does not fly down with the others but flaps and whirrs between the trees in a dazzle of white wings. As it turns gracefully above their heads Alvie cries "Oh look, Phil!" then laughs out loud as it comes to land in front of the child, a plastic wind-up toy. "I thought it was *real!*" And she links her arm in his and squeezes, a gesture that says Aren't I silly and isn't that bird silly and isn't all this *fun?*

As they get closer to the child scattering crumbs, Philip notices a very tall, very thin black man approaching. With one long arm the man scoops up the bird then stands quite still, not speaking to the child who has begun to stalk a real pigeon — not speaking to Alvie or Philip either, hardly looking at them in fact, but by the way he is standing as aware of them as they are of him. His thin black fingers caress the plastic toy. It is one of those moments, Philip thinks, one of those moments that means more than itself, the women's conversation that I can almost understand and the child hunting and the black man with the white bird, waiting. I'll buy it for Alvie as a memento, for fun.

As he hesitates, adding up *lire* in his head, he hears an Australian voice saying "Jesus, this world!" Turning, he finds a young man with a rucksack standing just behind him. "He does that every day," says the stranger, giving a nod towards the black man. "Him and dozens of others like him all over Europe. Haven't you seen them? They're slaves — yes, slaves," he repeats at Alvie's startled look. "There's a boss man somewhere around, he brings these people into the country and provides the bits of plastic and a shed for them to doss down in, and out they go, every day, tourists or no tourists, trying to earn a few cents because they're all wanting to get back home, especially now that winter's coming on and winter in Europe's not much fun if you come from a warm place but they haven't got a hope, they'll never earn their fare back again, the best they can hope for is enough to eat and a place to sleep and if they don't manage to sell any the boss man kicks them out and they starve."

On hearing this Philip thinks, I couldn't bear that bird now, I'll just *give* him the money. But as he struggles in his mind for the right words in Italian, *I want . . . I do not want*, the black man abruptly launches the plastic toy into the air and follows it to the other side of the piazza, and the opportunity is lost.

"We're off to see David," Alvie is saying to the stranger. "The Accademia's just around the corner."

The stranger nods. "Me too. I'll tag along with you." He shrugs his shoulders to ease the rucksack decorated with a blue and white Eureka flag, that symbol of freedom. He looks as though he's been travelling a long time. His boots are worn down to the uppers, his jeans in tatters, Philip observes, glancing down at his own neat jeans bought for this trip. His untrimmed beard and his hair tangling on to his shoulders make Philip think of a satyr, one of those hairy half-human creatures of woods and fields that he and Alvie have been looking at in dozens of paintings and sculptures over the last few days. Marsyas, he thinks. The satyr Marsyas — the one the painters loved because he challenged the god Apollo and got skinned alive. He hears Marsyas tell Alvie "David was carved out of the one big block of stone. They say that when Michelangelo looked at it he could see David there in it, waiting to get out."

"Is that so?" exclaims Alvie, opening her eyes wide — and Philip raises his eyebrows to himself, since it was only yesterday that Alvie herself read that bit of information out loud from a guide book in a bookshop.

*   *   *

Philip stands for a long time in front of Michelangelo's first Slave, one of four in the gallery, marvelling at the anguished effort in the powerful shoulders and stomach muscles as the imprisoned man struggles against his bondage of stone. Michelangelo never finished it, Philip thinks, but it looks just right the way it is — the figure trapped, straining, not whole yet, desperate to stand free like the David.

He looks around to tell Alvie . . . and sees that she has already finished looking at the four Slaves, and not only the Slaves but the highlight of the gallery, David standing in the floodlit niche. She is slouching with her back to the Pietà of Michelangelo's old age, the one Philip read makes an interesting comparison with the highly polished one in the Vatican. She is talking to the stranger.

Moving closer he hears her saying in the bantering tone that annoys her when other women use it to men: "Okay, so Jesus's legs are deliberately sculpted all rough, not even the same length, so you tell me why."

"Because Michelangelo was in a hurry, he was afraid he might die before he finished," Philip puts in quickly.

The stranger glances at him. "When people were crucified, hanging there was such agony they used to push up with their feet against the nail to get a few seconds' relief, so the soldiers would come around with clubs and break their legs so that they couldn't."

"*God!*" Alvie exclaims. "Why are people so *vile* to one another? . . . Did you know that?"

Philip shakes his head. "Have you had a good look at the David?" he asks as she makes to move towards the door.

The stranger, turning with her, says over his shoulder, "Take a look at David from the side. There's real apprehension on his face. You don't get that on the postcards."

Philip catches Alvie's eye. "Come and look?"

"No. You." She glances back at the half-formed torsos and the beaten corpse. "I'm going outside for a bit."

He shrugs, and takes longer than he means to over the rest of the sculpture. When he comes out of the gallery he finds her sitting alone on the steps.

"Let's go."

"Hang on," she says. "I'm minding his rucksack."

He notices it then, the grimy worn rucksack with the Eureka flag. "Is *he* still hanging around?"

"What's eating you?"

He says nothing to that, just sits beside her on the cold step and watches the black man throwing the plastic pigeon.

(V) Triptych

"This one," Alvie says, peering in through the window of the *locanda*. "All the people in here look like locals." An elderly waiter escorts them to a table and pulls out their chairs with a flourish. Alvie, laughing up at the man, insists on giving the three orders in her atrocious Italian. Three, because the stranger is still tagging along. Marsyas. The satyr with the Eureka flag. When Philip said to Alvie on the gallery steps "So let's get something to drink. Okay?" *he* said as he hoisted up his rucksack, "Good idea. What about something a bit more substantial?"

Philip mentally calculates *lire* again. One good meal a day. And a bottle of wine. He sees Eureka Flag top up his glass — tops up his own.

Eureka Flag is telling Alvie that he's on his way home. Back to an Australian summer. He's been wandering around Europe for months.

"I suppose you've been in every gallery and cathedral,"

Philip says enviously. It's the first thing he has said to him.

The guy says no he hasn't, as a matter of fact this is the first gallery he's bothered with, but he thought he'd better see something to tell his family. He doesn't go for this sort of thing as a rule, there are too many terrible things going on in the world to be wasting his time in old tombs and churches, we might all be blown up tomorrow the way things are heading.

"All the more reason," Philip replies, warming to the debate, "for seeing all this before it disappears . . . It doesn't seem logical not to," he continues eagerly. "I mean, here are all these marvellous things around you that have inspired people for centuries — ordinary people I mean as well as all sorts of artists — and either way you're going to miss out, aren't you? Either by being blown up, which might not happen anyway, or by worrying yourself silly beforehand —" And he gives him a rundown on all the things he's missing right here in Florence, the Loggia for instance, an open-air museum full of statues of old Greek legends, Hercules breaking a Centaur's neck, and the Rape of someone, two rapes actually, and Perseus with the head of Medusa. And the Baptistry doors — he mustn't miss the Baptistry doors, especially Ghiberti's, Paradise and murder and wrath and punishment in ten bronze panels.

Eureka Flag leans forward. "Centuries of it, right? See, I've got this theory —"

"And the Cathedral," Philip interrupts, splashing wine into their glasses. (Alvie puts her hand across hers.) "The Cathedral — there's another Pietà there, a polished one like the one in the Vatican." He racks his brains for something to cap the other's comment about the Pietà they saw this morning.

"What have you been doing?" Alvie asks.

He replies that he's just been to Germany for the autumn peace demonstrations. He was with the people blockading

one of the American missile bases. When they started the
blockade no one knew whether the police would play it low
key or get heavy. Boy, water cannon are no joke!

"It doesn't seem like you've been having much of a fun
time overseas," Alvie comments, wrinkling up her nose.
And she smiles at him. Chin propped on one hand. Smiling.

"Or achieving anything much," Philip adds, turning to
order more wine.

"Wrong!" says the guy. "People like you two should go
along to a demonstration sometime. See for yourselves. At
the missile base for instance. Boy, was that something! All
those blockaders working together, *caring* for each other,
it's the only way, getting together, showing people, it's true
what old JC said (not that I'm religious or anything like
that), Wherever two or three are gathered together — like
the three of us, say. That's all it takes because before long
two or three more will join in and soon you'll have a
crowd, you'll have a whole city, a nation — all because of
two or three. Only they've got to care, that first bunch,
they've got to get rid of all the fear inside themselves, all
the anger, they've got to love one another —" He smiles
apologetically. "Have you noticed how easy it is to say you
hate something, I hate the unions, but if you start on about
love everyone thinks you're some sort of nutter?"

Alvie says "I love Ronald Reagan," and laughs.

Philip tries to catch her eye: *We love each other*.

At that moment their meal arrives.

"That was quick," Eureka Flag comments. He grins at
Alvie. "It helps all right if you know the language."

Alvie gives a little shrug of pleasure, a quick tightening
of the shoulders like a hug. "And if you're a woman,"
Philip smirks.

"Oh rubbish!" Alvie says. "They just like you to try."

Philip lifts his glass and studies the dark red wine.

"Especially if you're a woman," he repeats, watching sideways as the colour runs into her face. He says softly, "It wouldn't matter how badly you said it."

Get stuffed! Alvie breathes.

Eureka Flag is saying "Great nosh-up, this. If I hadn't found you guys I'd have just grabbed a pizza somewhere." He says are they going to Germany, he can give them the name of friends to stay with in Germany, they're great people, they live in a huge old converted barn so there's heaps of room, they'll make Alvie and Philip welcome in Germany.

"Sounds great!" Alvie says. "Phil?"

"Are we going to Germany?" Philip responds in what comes back to him as the thin sarcastic tone he hasn't heard in years, his father's to his mother, before they split up. So he says hastily, "Yes, the Loggia — he must see the Loggia, mustn't he, Alvie? And just a few steps away there's David again." "A replica," Alvie explains. "The small force against the evil in the world!" Philip declaims, flourishing his glass. He adds "With bird shit on his head!" And laughs.

For a moment Alvie stares at him like a mother or something, then turns back to her plate. "How's yours?" she asks the other guy. "Want to try some of mine?" They exchange spoonfuls. Philip shrieks with silent laughter when a gob of pasta catches in his beard.

"Philip?"

"No thanks. I'm happy with what I've got."

"Well — can I have a taste, then?" Alvie persists. Philip shrugs, and pushes his plate across the table. She asks, concentrating on her fork, "Do you have brothers and sisters back home?" The guy's face lights up. Two sisters and a brother, he tells her. "Uhuh," says Alvie, nodding. She says "My Aunt Trudi's a teacher — you know? And she reckons you can always tell the kids without any brothers and sisters the day they come to school. They never want to lend their coloured pencils."

"Is that so?" says Philip.

(VI)   Commedia dell'Arte

Then Philip, emptying the bottle into his glass, hears himself saying so heartily that Alvie starts staring again, "So what are we all doing the rest of this afternoon? You could go to the Uffizi, mate, but it'll be closing time soon, and if you want to stick with us why don't we just walk around in the centre of town?" and Spaghetti Beard says "Great, mate!" so they're landed with him for the rest of the day. Philip, hogging the guide book, shouts "The Loggia! Let's start with the Loggia," but Marsyas the rebel jumps to his feet shouting "No, Paradise — that's where it all started, mate, all the aggro."

"Alvie?" says Philip.

Alvie sits scraping up the dregs of her cappuccino with her spoon. Suddenly she bursts out "So where's it all getting us? That's what I'd like to know. All this cruelty, snakes crushing people, men racing off women or fighting half-horse things, Judith cutting off some guy's head I don't know how many times, some poor young guy shot full of arrows and looking *pleased* about it for Chrissake! — It's horrible, horrible, I don't care if I never see another bleeding Jesus!"

They are silent for some minutes then. She goes on scraping the bottom of her cup until Philip has to stop himself reaching over and taking it from her because when he was a child his mother would never let him do that.

*   *   *

"Let's go back to the big square," suggests their companion. "There's usually something happening in the squares, even at this time of year." Street theatre, he tells them — he was into a bit of street theatre himself with the peace movement. Sure enough, in the piazza people are gathering around a young woman who has lighted some sort of flare in a tin and is blowing bubbles. Flickering light catches at the bubbles as they float off into the dusk. Two or three children run with upstretched arms. Suddenly the woman puts down the bubble pipe and reaching out catches one, two, three, four bubbles and begins to juggle them, her eyes dark pits in her uplifted face. A murmur runs through the crowd. Somebody claps. At the sound her hands falter. One of the bubbles drops and bounces once, twice on the pavement.

Leaning forward without looking down the woman catches the bubble and tosses it back with the others — gobs of colour pulled together into a pattern of light.

"Oh!" Alvie cries, delighted. "Now how does she do that?"

It's just what I'm trying to do with words, Philip thinks, or does he shout it, because Alvie and Spaghetti Beard begin to laugh, all around people are laughing, staring at him, and he burns with embarrassment, hearing himself sound pretentious, ridiculous. He hates her for joining in with that fellow in mocking him. He turns away quickly — and sees what they have all been guffawing at. It is not him at all, but a young man behind him, right at his shoulder, another of these street theatre characters, a mimic this time. Philip, turning, catches him leaning forward earnestly, just as Philip must have been leaning, a frightful frown on his face. As he turns the young man jumps away and begins to mince across the piazza behind a woman wearing extraordinarily high heels. Each time the woman half-glances over one shoulder, conscious of something out of place, the mimic steps to the other shoulder, so artful you can see those high heels on his mocking ankles. This time Philip joins in the laughter, even throwing a few hundred *lire* when the man brings around his cap, but the noise screams in his ears.

(VII) Love Lies Bleeding
or
The Muse Nailed

"Let's go!" he says as Marsyas moves off to look at the huge white Neptune dominating the piazza. Not yet, Alvie replies. He can if he wants, but there's plenty happening here, she's going to hang about for a bit.

"With him?"

"He's okay. He's nice. You stay too."

"What for? I can't see anything happening. Come on. I don't want to hang around any more."

She shrugs his hand off her arm. "Well maybe I do."

Marsyas comes back to them. "You two coming?"

He hovers indecisively. "I want to do a bit of writing," he says, looking at Alvie.

"Letters home," says Marsyas.

He would let it go at that but Alvie says "No, poems, he writes poems, he's working on something right now but he won't let anyone see till it's finished. He's good," she adds. "He gets things published."

"Only in things no one's ever heard of," he says modestly.

"What do you write about?"

"Love poems," Alvie replies as he hesitates, so that he feels himself going red again.

"You should write about real things," says Marsyas. "I mean, like what's going on around us in this stuffed-up world. The sort of things those guys —" He gestures towards the marble figures in the Loggia — "have been rabbiting on about for centuries. Only now it's pollution and Pershing missiles. Same thing, isn't it? You're good, she says — you might change something."

"I'll keep it in mind," Philip replies, furious with her, with both of them.

Back in the room at the *pensione* he sits on the bed under the bare globe and on a fresh page of his notebook writes *Art mocks Life*. Or should it be the other way around? *Life stuffs up Art*. Then he sits for a long time tapping the pencil. How can she just wander off till all hours in a foreign city with some yobbo she knows nothing about? *Satyr holds orgy in bed-and-breakfast*. *Sabine woman siezed, rescuer trampled*. He writes *Life* again then sits turning the pencil point in the dot over the i. The minute she sets foot in this room he will grab her, rip off leaves and bark to the heartwood, screw her till she screams, screw that satyr out of her, flay him alive in front of her, shoot her full of arrows, thorns, nails, break her legs —

He begins to write. The pencil races. When he has finished there appears a poem that leaves him drained and triumphant but is so ugly, so violent that as he rereads it he feels sick. Throwing pencil and notebook on to the floor he crawls into bed. He is awakened later — minutes? hours? — by muffled laughter, the turning of the door handle, more squawks of laughter. "Put the light on," he says coldly. "I'm not asleep." The glare almost blinds him but he can make her out, alive with laughter, and behind her, standing in the doorway clutching his rucksack, *him*.

"He's got nowhere to sleep," she says. "He had to vacate his room yesterday morning, so I said he could camp here overnight."

"Oh sure," he replies. "Help yourself. Room in this bed for three. Edge or middle?"

But sarcasm is wasted on *him*. "No worries, the floor's fine by me," says the satyr, and begins to unroll a thin grubby mat and a sleeping bag.

She titters again. "You should have heard me chatting up the guy on the desk so he wouldn't notice him sneaking upstairs!"

When he wakes again, head aching, groin aching, it is almost daylight. The intruder has gone. Mat, sleeping bag, rucksack — gone. He turns his head; Alvie is still asleep. As he slides his hand between her thighs she murmurs half-waking and puts her arms around him. When they have made love they turn back to back, their bottoms touching. From the edge of the bed he sees his notebook lying open on the floor, and remembers with amazement his poem of last night — too shameful to show anyone, too good to tear up. As light seeps into the room he can make out several pencilled arrows pointing to something scrawled under his own writing. Leaning out to reach it, he reads *Thanx!* and an address in Germany.

WHAT'S THE TIME, MR WOLF?

"Hey Jez. I know the grass man, Jez," Mollison drawls, wiping his mouth with the back of his hand. Gerald stares. What's the guy on about? Dope's been around forever. Three guys nearly got expelled last term. Gave the headmaster the shits worrying about nosy journos. "Fosters or Four X?" Mollison rolls another can along the counter towards Gerald. "Yup, any time, man. All the dope I want."

Gerald, fumbling with the ring-pull, nods. And the hard stuff too? Typical of Mollison. Access to everything. Like his father's bar fridge every day before his old lady gets in. Like the girl in the St Vinnie's dress sitting cross-legged on the floor, hands palm up on her knees. One of Mollison's groupies. Second year at high school. Love letters to Mollison from half a dozen of her classmates — Mollison reads them aloud in the Sixth Form common room. What *is* it about guys like Mollison? Catching the girl's eye Gerald thinks she's smiling at him, or maybe is going to smile. His mouth feels too small all of a sudden for the wires and his wayward teeth.

"Dentists kept telling my ol' lady all four of us kids needed braces," he babbles. "Buck teeth, bad bite, all the usual crap, you know? But guess who ended up with them. Because why? Because she's cunning, my ol' lady, dead cunning. She took the four of us together to the orthodontist and he said You want a package deal, do you? And *she* said —"

Mollison drains his can and tosses it behind the bar. "I *am* the grass man, man," he says.

"Balls," says Gerald, making an effort to straighten his shoulders. In the mirror behind the bar, the hair at the back of his head stands up like straw. His arms look like sticks. He tries flexing a muscle, and imagines himself arm-wrestling Mollison, forcing that slick arm right down to the counter top and holding it there easy as a twig.

"Balls," says Gerald again, sadly.

"Plenty that way too," Mollison snickers.

Gerald hears himself snickering back. He sways to his feet. He must have got through twice as much booze as Mollison. That's because as soon as the girl turned up Mollison dropped his cue in the middle of a shot, saying "Help yourself to the fridge, ol' man," and the two of them disappeared. Gerald feels a bit pissed off about that. Guest, he is a guest. Mollison actually phoned him. To play pool. Commiserate. The girl just turned up.

"Grass," Gerald mumbles. "I reckon you're just having me on."

"You want a bet?" Mollison slides off his bar stool. "Come out in the garden — not you," he adds to the girl as she turns her stalky neck towards him. "You better push off. My old woman'll be home soon."

"Jeez I'm fed up to here with that chick," he says to Gerald as soon as they are outside. He runs his hand edgewise across his throat.

"Why do you have her around so often, then?" Gerald sneers.

Mollison laughs. He drawls "Like it's free, man. It's free."

The late afternoon sun dances up and thumps Gerald

right between the eyes. "I'd like to be free," he mutters, thinking he can't take another year of this, catching two buses to and from Grammar and listening to Mollison's love life and rushing to hand in God-awful assignments yes sir no sir three bags full sir.

"Me too," Mollison says in the diffident voice Gerald hasn't heard since the day they first met, himself an old hand at Grammar by a whole term and Mollison the new kid given to him to look after. It took till lunchtime for Mollison to start acting as though it was the other way about, but right now Gerald pushes that niggle aside.

"Listen Tony," he says, the idea changing into top gear without a hiccup and bowling along sweetly at a touch. "No one knows this yet but I'm not going back to that dump, not ever. What's the point? Who's to say I'd do any better next time? As soon as the holidays are over I'm off. I'm going to head north. Thumb. I've heard there's places you can pick up jobs dead easy. Truck driving — I can drive a car. Prospecting. Cook — I reckon any fool could do that. Listen, why don't the two of us go together? You don't want to sit through this year again any more than I do."

"Why wait till the vacation's over?" Mollison asks, leading the way between beds of flowers. "Why not tomorrow?"

Gerald shrugs. "Dunno. Guess I was thinking after we get back from the coast. My old man's got a cottage booked down at the coast."

"Yeah?" Throwing his head back, Mollison studies Gerald from under eyelids like half-drawn blinds. "The coast. Holiday house at the coast. The annual exodus from the national treadmill. Broulee. Mossy Point. Pebbly Beach. The old man coming down on weekends to get pissed and the old lady making sure she's a candidate for skin cancer. Can't take your chick behind the sand dunes because you'll trip over some other shagger. Come February it's back to bells and blazers and try again for that little bit of paper. The world is your oyster bed, man. Nine to four in the classroom, nine to five in the office. Must keep your options open, son." Reaching sideways he pulls a dahlia head through his fingers and scatters the petals. "My old man's in Rio, you know that? Conference. He's got his dollybird with him. Keeping his options open. Same old roller-coaster, man."

"Yeah," Gerald agrees, trying to convince himself he's bored out of his brain with running at daybreak across squeaking sand to pit himself against the tall, chill water, or clambering around the slippery headland to frighten his sisters, or making a shadow over rock pools just to watch the sea anemones close then flower again in their blue-green pools.

"It's a gas, Jez," continues Mollison, the slick, the astute. "Soon as I sell what I've got growing over here by the back fence we can do it in style. Four star motels. All the pussy we want. Style, man! It's taller than me already. The female of the species grows taller than the male, you heard that before, Jez?"

"Don't *they* have anything to say?" Gerald asks, following Mollison along a path overhung with ripening peaches and apples. "About growing it here, I mean."

"The olds? Nah. Like it's a Mexican marigold, Jez. New hybrid. Anyway they leave everything to the gardener, and he leaves this back corner to me. No worries."

They stop at the edge of a bed of tomatoes, each vine neatly pruned and staked. Mollison waves his arm high in the air. "How's that?" he begins, then freezes. "What the —! It's *gorn!*"

The harsh green smell of crushed vines fills Gerald's nostrils as Mollison thrashes forward. He follows more carefully. Mollison is standing in a small patch between the tomatoes and the fence. At his feet is a ragged, fibrous stump about the width of a fist. "It musta been that sodding gardener!" Mollison shrieks. "Sodding ratbag! I oughta dob him in to the sodding pigs!"

He tears at the tomato vines. Jumps up and down. Runs through his vocabulary of curses and begins again. Gerald steps back as pulp and seeds spray.

"It'll be good to clear out from all this," he offers tentatively as they make their way back to the house.

"Yeah?" Mollison turns on him. "That's life, eh Jezza? Say la vee. Win some lose some. Bob up smiling again tomorrow. Is that what you're trying to say? Jeez mate, hasn't anyone ever *told* you?"

The girl is waiting for them on the back patio. Her cotton dress reaches to her ankles. Gerald can see right through it to her pink-tipped breasts, the curve of her hip, the tiny vee of her panties. "Your mother just rang, Tony," she says in her whispery voice.

"And you answered?" exclaims Mollison. "Dumb twat!"

"It was ringing and ringing, Tone. She said for you to fix yourself a salad with whatever's going in the fridge, don't wait for her, she's going to be late. Okay?" She hesitates. "I guess I'll be off now, Tone."

Gerald wants to say "I'm off now, too — maybe I can give you a lift?" He thinks the girl looks at him as though she would like him to say that. And he can't of course because all he has to get home on is his bicycle. Fat lot of good it was getting his licence the day he turned seventeen.

Mollison is saying "What's all the hurry?" He goes up to the girl and slides his arm around her waist. Gerald sees his hand lay hold of her breast, two fingers pincer her nipple.

He looks away. Across the valley the Brindabellas are such a thick, flat blue that they look like cardboard cutouts pasted on to the sky. Earlier, cycling to Mollison's, he could pick out every feature, rocky outcrops, hollows, the grey scalp of soil under the gum trees, the tight green patches of pine where the guys ride trail bikes. The old Brindies, never the same, always changing.

"See you," he says.

By the time he reaches home it is almost dinner time. As he expects, the old Mercedes, the car he learned to drive on because the Range Rover's an automatic, is in the garage; that means his mother is home. The Range Rover isn't beside it — his father must be working late again. In the family room his sisters are watching a serial. Gerald leans over each chair in turn, wishing they would take their eyes off the convulsing screen for even a moment because soon when he and Mollison are driving bulldozers out in the desert they might be sorry they haven't. "Shove off, Gerry, your breath stinks," one of the girls says, without lifting her gaze. The second girl twitches her shoulder. The youngest one chants "I know something you don't, Gerry, Gerry, I know where to find magic mushies in the Brindies. Gerry?"

"*Mushies*," mocks Gerald. "*Brindies*." He goes into the dining room. Taking the sherry decanter from the sideboard he unstoppers it and takes several swigs, then fills it to its original level from the jug of water someone always sets on the dinner table.

His mother is in the kitchen. As she looks up to greet him he announces loudly that in no way can they get him to repeat his final year, he has made up his mind to spend the next six months bumming around Australia.

She has no reasoned-out reply to that. She just puts down the half-drained saucepan she is holding over the sink and says after a moment, "That needs a bit of thinking about, Gerry."

The good smells of dinner seize Gerald like a cramp. Why the hell is the old man late every night? He clutches at the sink and turns unsteadiness into a shrug. "So? What is there to think about?"

His mother smiles. It is a crazy smile. It doesn't belong to her face. It spins off the copper-based saucepans and goes leaping all over the kitchen.

Gerald says "What's wrong with your mouth?"

"*Pardon*, Gerry?" She peers at him, frowning.

"I know what you mean," he begins. "I know what you're going to say." He can hear someone's voice growing louder and louder. "Keep your option, options open — I don't give a stuff about *options*."

"*Barley*, Gerry," she says, as though they are two little kids in the playground and she's calling halt. She adds "Were you over at Tony Mollison's this afternoon?"

He stares in amazement at the amount of pepper her hands are shaking into the soggy potatoes. She ought to drain them properly and he wants to do it for her, poor old Mum, but the stove and the sink keep retreating whenever he looks at them and then, as he turns his head, creeping up on him again. Like that kids' game. How did it go? "What's the time, Mr Wolf?" "Two o'clock." Behind Mr Wolf you take two steps forward. "What's the time, Mr Wolf?" "Eight o'clock." Eight steps. Gerald can still feel the thrill of fear. "What's the time — ?" and before you can tig him Mr Wolf springs around on you shouting "*Dinner time!*" . . . Poor old Mum. Trapped all her life in a crazy kitchen.

"That's what you should have done, Mum. Hitched around Australia. Seen a bit of the world."

"Oh Gerald." She laughs. Her face swings back into focus. "But it's a good idea for you," she is saying. "A young chap going off on his own, going adventuring. Fantastic, Gerry! Can I use your new tape deck while you're away? You can't carry much in a rucksack. Have you got a rucksack? You *have* thought about a rucksack, Gerry? And that old sleeping-bag. A bit thin now, isn't it? It can get pretty chilly at night by the side of the road. And boots.

Comfortable boots. Did you remember to get yours resoled? Maybe if someone picks you up they'll let you take a turn at driving. Isn't it good you persevered with your licence?" It was she who would haul him out of bed so that he could practise on the Mercedes with her beside him before she rushed back to see to breakfast and school lunches. "Cash," she is saying. "Have you considered Keycard, Gerry? It's very convenient. On the other hand —"

Gerald feels his resolution breaking up like the soft cords of potato oozing through the holes in the masher.

"Stuff you, Mum!" he shouts. "I was trying to tell you something!"

They are both so shocked at this outburst that when she says "I think you'd better go to your room," he goes without protest. By leaving his bedroom door open, he is able to overhear her tell his father that he isn't feeling well, probably upset about his exam results.

"Should bloody well think so!" he hears his father reply. "Whole damn' year down the drain. Not to mention what I paid out in fees. That's gratitude for you — Pass the water jug, Helen. Spud's a bit hot, isn't it? — So what does he plan to do with himself this coming year? Bludge on us for another twelve months? You know what I'd like to do? Throw the lot to the wolves — no, not the dinner, Helen — all these dropouts. Let them see how they get on on their own. Sort a few sheep from the goats that way, maybe."

Gerald's heart beats so hard as he waits for his mother to announce the hitchhiking plan that he misses whatever it is she says next.

His father is saying "But *why* can't he pass his exams first off? Christ, when I was his age I'd been working for my old man for three years — no second bite at the cherry then, by God!" Gerald has to snigger at his father's choice of phrase.

When his ears creep up on his parents again his father is

trotting out the old heavies: recession, depression, dole bludgers.

It's a conversation that has prowled around the dinner table so often that he doesn't listen any more but pulls the bedclothes over his head and in the smirky darkness strips that art teacher with the big tits who is always at them to get something finished. "Relax Miss, there's always next year, we'll be back," they drawl, just to see her boobs rock with anger in her tight pink sweater. Like that time, leaning over Gerald's chair, she told Mollison he'd be better off looking for a job instead of wasting everyone's time at school and he answered in that little-boy voice he reserves for women teachers, "I did leave, Miss, I got two jobs gardening and I got the sack from both of them so I come back here, Miss." Oh brother! If only Gerald had raised his head he'd have collided with that pair of bazongas. *See you next year, Miss!* Gerald has to come up for air, raising his head above the bedclothes just in time to hear his father say "You spoil him, Helen."

"But look at it this way, Bob, it might be an incentive to work. Driving the Mercedes to school every day instead of catching two buses or pushing that bike. He's not stupid, Bob. And so close to getting there. I don't mind doing without a car this year if it's going to help him get through."

Goddam the cunning bitch! First thing tomorrow he'll get over to Mollison's and they'll get stuck into their plans for the north.

He ought to drive over. Get in some practice. He needs that practice all right if he's going to front up to some boss waving his driver's licence. Over breakfast he'll ask his mother if she'll lend him the Mercedes for the day. She's sure to say yes. His heart lurches as though he's run into the gutter, then hammers like a cracked muffler. *Why come home again? Why not hop in the car and keep on*

driving until he and Mollison are miles from anywhere?
Goondiwindi, Tibooburra, Thargomindah . . .

Then he remembers that Mollison will be sure to have
some chick with him. Some new groupie, some hitchhiker
who's taken a shine to him. It will be today all over again,
the two of them disappearing and Gerald hanging about
waiting. In his mind's eye he sees exactly how it will be,
miles of sandhills and himself standing hatless beside some
tin shed picking bindis out of his feet . . . Well stuff
Mollison! He can do without Mollison. Just ask the old
lady at breakfast for a lend of the car. Get in a bit of practice. Oh brother! He sees himself come February rolling up
to school in the old Merc and everyone's eyes popping and
after school all the chicks queueing up and Mollison's
chick first in the line, her nipples thrust at him pink as
cherries and the shiverygrass voice whispering *Free,*
Gerry . . .

THE WOMAN AT THE WINDOW

Sharon takes out another cigarette and reaches for the lighter. Today, before she catches sight of Mickey again, she is letting herself use the lighter; after that it's matches. It's one of her good luck things. She's standing by the kitchen window but she can't take anything in yet because she's still shaking. Thank God people in the other flats wouldn't have heard, they'd have left for work. When Mickey nags it's not a soft mosquito's whine like little Trace but a piercing shriek, as though she's belting the life out of him when she's never so much as laid a finger!

"*Stop* it, Mickey!" she hisses as the sound goes on echoing in her head. She touches her shin. It's going to come up like one of those purple and green eggfruits where the little devil's heel caught her. She grabbed his arms and pushed them into his jacket, the one he ripped but it's got his name and address pinned on to it, then she dragged him, roaring and flailing, out to the landing and gave him a push towards the stairs. "Get lost, Mickey!"

She jabs out her cigarette in a dirty cup. It's matches now — she can see Mickey's bobbing blonde head. He's fine, he's just fine. Arms spread like wings, he's scattering dozens of magpies as he runs across the grassed area between the flats and the church centre. His sneakers will be soaked again. There's a perfectly good path but he never remembers. Sometimes a man comes on a toy tractor and mows the grass. Squawk park, Sharon calls it, because of all the magpies flapping and clamouring and poking their beaks down one another's throats. Now Mickey's stalking one of the parent birds. Walking just ahead of him, the magpie keeps one eye on him and one on the grass. A young bird flies clumsily towards it, overshooting the spot and landing yards away. You often see them dead on the ring-road. Mickey watches the parent run to feed the squawking baby, then himself continues to run, arms outspread, towards the flats.

The magpies nest in the trees overhanging the flats and some of the residents feed them. It stops them swooping, the woman in the adjacent flat tells Sharon. She corners Sharon one morning on the landing, just as Sharon is about to close her door on Mickey and the woman is coming out of hers, all rugged up against the sharp August morning and clutching a plastic bag full of something soft and oozing. Chopped up rump, she tells Sharon. I feed them every morning on my way to work, she says. Sharon ducks her head; the memory of her voice is as sharp as a beak. They don't like mince, the woman says, even though Sharon's door is three-quarters shut by this time and Sharon is staring over her head at a patch of blue sky through the landing window. I told the butcher, I said That says something about the quality of mincemeat, doesn't it, when the magpies refuse to eat it!

Maybe if they swooped a bit more the ranger would come and shoot a few! Sharon says, or thinks about saying. After that morning she's careful never to open her door at the time the woman will be leaving for work, not even if Mickey's teasing baby Tracey or demanding more Cocopops or screaming till Sharon's head bursts.

I could ring the ranger myself, Sharon thinks, hurrying from the kitchen to the living room where the window looks on to the ring-road. There's a phone box below her, next to the pedestrian crossing. She sees herself going down the landing stairs and around the corner, pushing the phone box door inwards so that it folds up on itself like a trick door and dropping in the coin and then the ranger coming with his gun bang! bang! He's wearing his smart ranger uniform and Mickey's off playing somewhere — standing by the pedestrian crossing actually, with his hand on the button. In the palm of her own hand Sharon feels the button beating like a slow loud heartbeat. *This time, this time, this time.* The baby's still asleep in Sharon's bed — no, Mickey's cot, it would have to be Mickey's cot — and she says I have always admired that uniform would you care for a sherry . . . only she drank the last of it yesterday, the empty bottle is lying in the middle of the living room. Would you care for cocoa? — cocoa because she's run out of tea and coffee, milk too she remembers, Mickey had that on his Weetbix. Sure would! says the ranger. I have always admired —

But, Sharon interrupts herself, how can I make that call, is it still twenty cents or has that box been changed over to thirty? Is it twenty or thirty? And she twists her hands in her nightdress until it tears a bit more at the shoulder.

Mickey is still standing by the crossing. He's swinging his foot at a dead baby magpie squashed on the ring-road. Every time a car rushes past, its feathery wings blow as though it is trying to fly. Traffic is heavy at this time of day. A stream of cars is pouring into the car park. The signal on the crossing changes from red to green, then back to flashing red. As people from the flats hurry across towards the shops and offices of the city centre, Sharon feels a surge of excitement. The drunks on the seat under the elms at the corner have been shopping already. This time the big man is carrying the paper bag. He places it carefully between his feet, opens a bottle, drinks and passes it to the next man. One of them starts to laugh, bending over then flinging back against the seat until the others join in, rocking backwards and forwards and slapping one another's shoulders. The big man grabs the bottle and, putting it to his mouth, holds it high like a trumpet.

Stragglers on the crossing scurry as the light turns red. Mickey isn't with them. He is pushing between the road edge and the low hedge in front of the flats. Sharon can see his bright curly head through gaps where the hedge has died. His hair curls on to his shoulders. It's like Rob's, soft and fair, whereas Tracey's is straight and dark like Peter's. It was Peter who helped her get this flat. You're in luck, he said. Most people have to wait months. Peter doesn't know about Tracey. He's working in Sydney now.

Sydney, Sharon says, and feels a wave of nostalgia, bitter as morning sickness. Sydney is sand and tanning oil, and your thoughts melting like ice-cream. Sydney is your sisters chatting up that lifesaver with the gold crucifix while you whined Come *on*, Mum'll get mad! Sydney is voices creeping out from broken tiles, Come on Shar, come and have fun!

That's how she met Rob.

It was at a party. There was this guy down from Canberra. He kept looking at Sharon. His eyes felt like hands on all the secret parts of her body. Sharon's friend shouted Who wants a ride on Rob's Harley Davidson? When it was Sharon's turn she heard herself saying Why don't we keep going till we get to Canberra? and that made Rob laugh. You'd like Canberra, he said. Sharon pictured a big white Parliament House surrounded by enormous houses with curving drives and huge green lawns where no one had to fight over whose turn it was in the bathroom. They arranged to meet the next day. It was Rob's last day in Sydney. She rode on the back of the Harley to a quiet beach where Rob had to see some people. Sharon thought she would go mad if Rob didn't keep touching her. She thought Rob's friends looked at her funny; didn't talk much in front of her. Try this, Rob said, passing her a thin, damp cigarette. They lolled around on the sand while the sun roared over them like gigantic surf.

When she returned home her mother, who thought she had gone into town for the day to look for a job, took one look at her and screamed "Don't start telling me a pack of lies, I don't want to hear it!" The next morning, while her parents were still sleeping, she stuffed what clothes she could into her old school haversack, stole her mother's collection of Charles and Di fifty cents and climbed out the bedroom window. She could have walked out the front door but the window seemed right. At Central Station she bought a ticket to Canberra and she hasn't been back home since, not once, nor written, nor telephoned.

"God, this place!" Sharon exclaims, turning her back to the window. There's a new stain on the sofa, and Mickey must have been at the horsehair again; it looks like a little animal trying to hide. Panic washes into Sharon's throat like a scummy tide. There are dirty cups on the TV and the floor and the window ledge; how long is it since she washed up? She seizes the empty sherry bottle; rushes cups, plates, baby's bottles and cutlery into the sink and pours cold water on to them; snatches up all the clothes she can find on the floor, over chairs, under the bed, never mind if they're dirty or not, she doesn't waste time looking — out, out they go, into the laundry basket. If they all go in, she thinks, if they all go in and nothing falls on the floor, *it will mean good luck*. Sometimes she starts off the day like that: if a bird flies past the window . . . if Mickey wakes up before Tracey . . . or it might be the other way round, if

Tracey wakes up before Mickey. The last thing, Mickey's bottom sheet that he's wet again, catches over the edge of the basket and hangs there, touching the floor but not falling either. Sharon's hands are shaking. She needs another cigarette. She's using the lighter again; that's allowed now.

She's down to her last cigarette. There are plenty in the shops of course, milk too, cigarettes and milk and the other things she has run out of. The shops are on the other side of the car park and the car park is on the other side of the ring-road and the ring-road is on the other side of the window.

She has to look away quickly.

She looks away to the seat under the elms where the drunks sit all day, even on days as nippy as this. She has a little fantasy that Rob is one of the men on the seat. Any minute now he'll look up and wave and she'll lock the kids in the flat and go down and they'll share the bottle or maybe a joint. It couldn't be any colder under the elms than it was in midwinter in the garage where she lived with him when she first came to Canberra.

Canberra was ace! Rob took her to parties and gigs or they stayed in the garage smoking hash or cuddled inside two sleeping bags zipped together, or they went over to the house where people were always coming and going. She never got to like the people in the house as much as Rob did; they talked to him more than they talked to her, and they'd bang hard on the bathroom door when she was daydreaming under the shower. Also they never cleaned up the kitchen, no one did except herself. Annie, the other girl who lived there, said "I don't know why you do it." But then Annie ate out; she could afford to, she had a job. She was a very bossy sort of girl, *woman* she insisted on, she hated *girl*. Sharon took to going over to the house only when Rob did, even if she was bursting, or she'd hang on till night time and squat behind the fig tree.

*   *   *

At first she thought it was just her body playing a trick. Rob said "Shit! You'd better do something, Shar!" and gave her six brand-new fifty dollar notes but she kept on putting it off, she got scared, she kept hoping her mother would write or just turn up on the doorstep.

And after a while it was too late.

Rob left Canberra soon after that. He said it was what they'd been talking about all winter, him and her zipping north on the Harley. He's back again now; he does the lighting for a new theatre group just up the road at Gilmore House. He stopped her one day when she was taking the two kids for a walk. "Sharon! How's things?" He's even been around once with a huge Mickey Mouse for Mickey, but when Sharon said "What about some regular maintenance, Rob?" he laughed. He said "You must be joking, Shar. I'm on the dole."

It was Annie who put her up to saying that to Rob. Annie's at Gilmore House, too — she's part of a women's video group — and she drops in at the flat sometimes for coffee. She drinks dandelion coffee so she brings her own. When Annie's talking, Sharon nods and says Yes Annie, yes, I should do that. Get your name on the waiting list for a three-bedroom house, Annie tells her. You're eligible, Sharon. When Rob cleared out, Annie persuaded her to move into a group house with Annie and two other women. They brought Sharon cups of herbal tea to stop the retching. They massaged her temples. They showed her articles about the effects of smoking on the developing foetus. They said You'll have no trouble getting family day care, Sharon, that's one of the good things about Canberra. They wanted her to have the baby in the house, with everyone helping. They began to talk about "our baby". One afternoon, while someone was practising on the drum kit in the living room, Sharon got dressed, climbed out her bedroom window and caught a bus into the city. In the city she did two things; she booked herself in at the hospital, and put her name down for a government flat.

The baby Tracey totters into the living room. She is crying, slow tears washing down her face like July rain. She's wearing an old pyjama coat of Mickey's, so shrunken her arms stick out to the elbows. Her napkin and plastic pants have fallen around her knees. Sharon pulls the napkin right off, then, sliding down to the floor, takes Tracey on to her lap and puts her to her breast. Tracey is going on two but if Sharon tries to wean her she cries, not a full-blooded roar like Mickey but *NnnnNnnn* like an insect trapped against glass.

When Mickey was starting to walk Sharon tried to get a job, a cash-paying job so as not to lose her pension. Cleaning, she thought. Annie wrote her a reference. Every Saturday she bought the paper and went through the Sit. Vac. The first lady she cleaned for asked her not to bring Mickey again, "little sticky fingers", so Sharon left him locked in the flat until one of the neighbours said that he cried and Sharon got scared of losing her lease. The second lady worked during the day so there were no worries there about taking Mickey. Sharon had the run of the house, she could dream out the windows, gaze all she wanted to at the pool and the green lawns, the mountains so sharply blue they made her throat wobbly, the fledgeling new Parliament House with its seven cranes bending down to it. Two days after starting work for this lady she received a letter: "Dear Sharon, Here is the money I owe you. I shall not be requiring you again. I wonder my dear if you have ever cleaned a house before? . . ." Sharon cried. She thought Tracey wasn't showing yet but the third lady said "You wouldn't be able to continue for long, would you dear? I'm very sorry but I really want somebody permanent."

"It isn't fair!" exclaims Sharon, putting Tracey aside and jumping to her feet. "It's all right for you!" she declares, staring at someone invisible across the room. Tracey tugs at her nightdress. Sharon snatches her up and thrusts her back at the breast, but the baby twists her head away. "Go down on the floor then, Tracey," Sharon sighs. She can't get over how different girls are from boys, even kids this age; when Mickey's inside he's at her all the time for Weetbix, fizzy drinks, biscuits. "What *is* it? Stop it, Trace. You want more titty? Trace?" She bends to lift her once again, but the child slips out of her grasp and, going into the centre of the room, falls to the floor and cries, *NnnnNnnn. NnnnNnnn.*

Sharon goes into the bedroom and closes the door. Stumbling over Mickey's broken tip-truck she discovers her purse on the floor, so she sits on her bed and empties it into her lap. She puts the five dollar notes on one side of her, the twos on the other; with the coins she makes a little tower that keeps falling over. After a while she peeps into the living room. Tracey has fallen asleep on the floor. Sharon picks her up and puts her into Mickey's unmade cot and pulls the side up. Heaving at it, she feels sick again, and remembers that she hasn't eaten anything since yesterday lunchtime when she finished off Tracey's tin of chicken dinner.

At the back of the refrigerator she finds a slice of bread in its plastic wrap. As she eats it at the kitchen window she watches the magpies in squawk park. The parent birds jab at wriggling things underground, run to the nearest begging baby, run run run on legs like twigs to find more food. The baby birds never stop pestering. Sometimes one of the parents gets really bossy, standing over a young one until it shuts up and pretends dead. Suddenly they all fly up into the trees. Two women and two children are coming along the path. One of the women is much older than the others; she is the mother, Sharon decides. The other woman is younger than herself, a girl really. She is swinging a man's purse by its wrist strap, and she isn't wearing a parka and beanie and scarf like the others, but a coat patterned with great zigzags of colour, red, green, purple, gold.

The mother and the girl in the coat stop to study a map. Visitors to Canberra, Sharon thinks, just as she once was. A tiny bubble of excitement surfaces. The visitors disappear around the corner of the flats and she runs to the living room window to see them reappear by the road. While they are waiting for the green light she tiptoes into the bedroom and pulls on her Indian cotton dress and the thick woollen cardigan that Annie gave her. She stuffs her money into her purse and hurries back to the living room window. There they are; the light has turned green but they are not crossing. *They are waiting for her*.

Mickey is still there between the hedge and the road, jumping on the spot as the cars fly past. Maybe he's said something cheeky to the family because as Sharon watches, the mother pushes past the hedge and speaks to him. He's not listening to her at all, jump jump jump, Sharon can feel those little pounding feet in the back of her head. She'll give him such a belting if he's been swearing again! The mother edges back to the others and speaks to the younger woman, the girl. The two kids giggle. The girl looks up at the flats, shrugs, then, although the light is angry red, turns her back on her mother and stalks across the road. Sharon feels a hot wave of excitement. When the light is green again the others cross too. Now the mother and the girl seem to be having a row. They stand under a pine tree in the car park, the woman pointing back at the flats and waving her arm and the girl staring down at the ground, sulky, Sharon decides, a bad girl, a runaway. Finally the woman and the two kids return to the lights and cross back towards the flats, but whether the girl follows Sharon doesn't wait to see. She didn't want the family to fight. She goes into the kitchen and puts the kettle on. There's a used teabag on the sink. Maybe she can squeeze another cup out of that.

The doorbell rings. That little shit Mickey! She's told him once this morning that there aren't any biscuits. He must have found a chair somewhere to stand on to reach the bell, must have dragged it all the way up the stairs. RR-Ring! RRRing! If she doesn't answer, if she holds her breath and pretends he's not there, he'll give up and go away again. She hears him ring the bell of the flat next door. The cheek of him! Pity the magpie woman's not home to give him what for.

She lights her last cigarette and goes back to the living room window. The family is still there, all four of them. They're standing by the phone box with their heads together. The mother goes into the box and after a moment comes out. The girl fiddles about in her purse and hands her something, a coin, Sharon supposes, then moves off a short distance, not quite part of the family and not separate either. The mother goes back into the box, leaving the door open. The two kids poke their heads in and listen.

Mickey's down there with them. He's holding on to his doodle and if she's told him not to do that she's told him a dozen times. Before she has time to think she hurries downstairs and around the corner.

"Get upstairs, Mickey."

The mother is out of the phone box by now, the two kids at her elbows.

"Excuse me," says the mother. "Is this your little boy?"

The girl in the bright coat comes a bit closer at this.

It takes Sharon a few moments to register that the woman is speaking to her. "Yes?" she says, abrupt and questioning at the same time. The girl and the mother exchange glances. The two kids are staring. Sharon pulls Annie's cardigan closer.

"He was standing — jumping — right on the edge of the road," the mother begins, as though she wants someone, the girl, Sharon, to take over.

"Yes?" Sharon repeats.

"The traffic's pretty heavy," the girl tosses in, then stares over everyone's heads as though it's all nothing to do with her.

"And that pretty fair hair," the mother adds eagerly, so that Sharon thinks Bet you wish yours was still the same! "He's so pretty," the mother is saying, "I mean I didn't realise he *was* a boy until I saw his name pinned on his jacket."

"And his address," puts in one of the kids importantly. "That's how we knew . . ."

Sharon says slowly "Well what business is it of mine?"

Their faces crumble with doubt. "But he *is* your little boy?" the girl asks, while the mother echoes "This is your mummy, darling?"

"Of course he is!" Sharon snaps. She adds "He knows about going out on the road. I've told him. He knows."

"But playing right on the edge — !" says the girl, while the mother cries "Such a pretty child! Someone might snatch him away!"

"Then it'll be his own fault, won't it?" retorts Sharon. "If he goes out on the road it'll be his own fault. He knows!" cries Sharon. "I've told him! You get along upstairs, Mickey!"

On the stairs she keeps saying "Hurry up, hurry *up*, Mickey!" She adds "You heard what those two said — if you're not a good boy someone will try to steal you!"

"*They* did!" wails Mickey. "That old lady tried to steal me! She telled the other one she would give me to a policeman. She said Come on, Mickey, you come with me. And the other one said —"

But what the runaway girl said Sharon doesn't hear, because at that moment the door bell rings again. This time, since it can't be Mickey, she opens it at once. On her doorstep, sharp as a mountain peak in his trim blue uniform, stands a policeman.

He says to Sharon, "Good morning, madam. Madam, we have just had a phone call . . ."

Sharon stands at the window. Through a dead patch in the hedge she can see Mickey clearly. As his mouth opens she stuffs her fingers in her ears but she can't shut out the bellow. Her hand is still smarting. As though he can't bear to stand still Mickey jumps up and down, up and down, jump jump jump jump, he jumps out into the road and as a car whizzes by he jumps back against the hedge, out and back, out and back —

This time! shrieks a voice in Sharon's head. *This time, Mickey, this time, this time!*

SETTLE DOWN COUNTRY

For days now, sand has blown through Myrrlumbing. People, walking to the springs or over the dunes or across Lake Alba to Lloyd's camp, hunch sideways, hugging their shoulders. Eyes and noses run red with grit. In the school building — a tin roof over chicken wire and spinifex walls — the teachers say "Okay people, no more lessons till the wind drops, eh?" *No name* Smith and Wilga say it in language, Robin and Dale in English. "*Yu*," they answer, children and older people brushing flies from their faces. "*Yu*." Yes.

Lloyd, sleeping behind the waist-high wall of spiny spinifex that Rhyll cut her hands gathering and packing, has to shake grit out of his sheets and blanket two or three times through the night, and each morning wakes with his tongue as parched as the dry salt bed of Lake Alba.

That bloody food truck should get here today.

There should be a letter.

Clear as the night sky, where planets are as bright as moons, he sees Rhyll climbing down from the cabin of a Haulpak. Between them stands the thick wall of spinifex but he can see right through it, can see like a cutout each salt wattle and tamarugo tree growing around the springs, can see the sleeping camps of the community, the dazzling lake bed, the bloodwood on the furthest dune. Rhyll, driving a ninety-tonne ore carrier a day and a half's drive away at Glencoe Goldmine — Rhyll has come back. She has left the engine running. She stands beside the front wheel, the top of her head barely higher than the axle. Hi, Lloyd! She takes a step towards him. Inside his camp, saucepans, tool kit, gas lamp all grow sharp in the half-light. He lifts his head. Rhyll vanishes. All he is left with is the faint roar of a truck. He shudders. He has been looking at a ghost girl.

He is wakened properly by a child shouting "Truck's comin', Lloyd! Truck's comin'!" Half a dozen voices take up the chant: *Truck's comin'! Truck's comin'!* The whine of its engine is distinct. It is crossing the dry bed of the Myrrlumbing River, creeping in bottom gear up the sandy incline. Boys' eager faces peer down at him. "Get up, Lloyd, truck's comin'. Lazy bugger." "Off my garden, you're trampling the gourds," he grumbles. Giggling, they all run off except Dexter, whose ears are still bad in spite of the big operation down south. "Off the gourds, mate!" Dexter nods, crunching the vines as he jumps up and down. "By the little spring now, I reckon. You get up, Lloyd!"

The food truck. It was due two weeks ago, but an hour out of town an axle broke and they had to fly parts up from the city. It will bring food for the next three weeks, gas for the four big refrigerators — letters. He jumps out of bed, savouring the early morning coolness. Later in the day the temperature will climb into the high forties. In the other camps people are already busy, lighting cooking fires, carrying buckets and billies to taps amongst the salt wattles. Fresh water comes from a series of springs. The springs are the lifeblood of the community. They are small holes in the sand where Myrrlumbing touched the earth as he flew across the desert. Where his shadow fell, lakes formed. The river ran. Kangaroos, turkeys, lizards were in plenty. No one ever went hungry.

Taking the larger saucepan, Lloyd goes out to his tap under the tamarugo trees. He has slept in again, working until God knows what hour when everyone else is asleep and he has a clear go. No one needing to sit down and talk business, no one wanting help with a sand-bogged vehicle. Also by midnight it's cooler in the office, the small room with a tin roof and spinifex walls at the back of his camp. Lloyd is the community coordinator, engaged by the desert people at Myrrlumbing to consult, listen, negotiate, suggest — and above all keep the bloody books up to date.

For the five weeks Rhyll was with him, she helped with the books.

He sloshes water over his face and neck and, as he does every morning, stands for a moment looking around him. Between his camp and the camps south of the low sand dune is the tip of Lake Alba, the most easterly in the Amaranth lake chain. This morning a haze of salt is drifting along Lake Alba. The sun is a huge inflamed eye. Dust hides the bloodwood on the horizon. He climbed it once. He and Rhyll went for a walk to satisfy themselves that what looked like a tree rising out of this strange red landscape really was a tree. He discovered a stone in the fork of two limbs, put there by whom, he wondered, looking about him then climbing down quickly.

All around them, under their light covering of spinifex, the dunes lay like resting limbs.

It was soon after their walk that Rhyll set about extending the spinifex walls around Lloyd's camp. His predecessors hadn't bothered. They were content with spinifex packed against chicken wire around the office, and shade cloth around the kitchen and sleeping area. Rhyll said being so open made her nervous. There was no *end* to anything. She could feel things wandering about. Bullshit, Lloyd said. They had their first argument. One night they were startled by the camp dogs suddenly barking, then a whoosh of flame. "Ghost feller," Simon Pepper explained the next morning. "Kerosene scare him off." Rhyll shot Lloyd a triumphant look: *ghost fellers!*

Well, she should feel safe now, walls all around her in the cabin of her Haulpak.

He throws a couple of saucepans of water on to the bottle gourds. She planted them. He forgot to water them yesterday.

People are running along the low dune. Very soon the truck will come over the dune, past Robin's and Dale's camps, past the store manager's garden, past the black, red and yellow flag signifying the people, the land and the sun. It will pull up beside the Portacoms, transportable sheds that came up from the city on trucks. One Portacom is the community craft centre, radio room and flying doctor's clinic; the community has been talking about purchasing separate buildings. The other Portacom, on which someone has painted silhouettes of hands, like a modern rock painting Rhyll said, is the store. Here they keep as much meat, fruit and vegetables as they can cram into the big gas refrigerator, and non-perishable things like flour and rice and soap powder.

Lloyd hurries into his camp and puts water to heat on the gas ring. There isn't time now to cook porridge. He stuffs a handful of oatmeal into his mouth and chews.

"Give us a lift with the generator, Lloyd, will you?" A small, wiry white man of fifty, maybe sixty, is talking at Lloyd before he is through the doorway. It is Marshall, the store manager, one of those people who have been around the outback for years. The people at Myrrlumbing call him that bluefeller, because of his hundreds of tattoos. Hearts, arrows, torsos, "Mother" — there isn't a square inch of me left, he told Rhyll. Want a little bet, darlin'? "That generator," he is saying to Lloyd. "It goes back with the truck, remember? You never showed up last night."

"I did, as a matter of fact, but your light was off." Dry oatmeal sprays as Lloyd speaks. "It was pretty late — I got stuck into the accounts."

"Jesus, those books! Forget it, finish your breakfast, I'll get Ernie Pilbara's boys." Marshall strides out, followed closely by Tuckey, a cattle dog with glaring yellow eyes that eats off Marshall's plate. They leave Lloyd thinking I should have gone over earlier last night, I should get through the bookwork quicker. That bloody dog!

He did his block with Marshall one evening while Rhyll was here — yelled at him to stop Tuckey sneaking food off her plate. Putting his arm around the dog's neck, Marshall said "Let's not have a fallin' out over possessions, mate, not here, not at this place," and went on talking about the potholes in the airstrip.

Maybe that's why Rhyll left.

She got a lift into town with the part-Aboriginal batik teacher who spent several weeks out at Myrrlumbing. It was a good time, those few weeks. Each evening one of them — Lloyd, Rhyll, Robin, Dale, the batik teacher or Marshall — would cook dinner for the other five. A leg of lamb in the Dutch oven if the food truck had just come in. Rice. Damper. Tomatoes and capsicums and rockmelons from Marshall's garden that he nurtures under shade cloth. They usually ate later than the other camps. Long after all the other lights and cooking fires were out, and the only sound was the occasional bark of a dog, the six of them would sit outside talking, arguing, watching shooting stars or picking out the Magellanic clouds like dust on a polished table, Marshall outraged by some Departmental cock-up, all of them excited, slapping at mosquitoes, throwing another piece of salt wattle on to the fire, their eyes weeping in the acrid smoke.

Yes, good times, all right.

The truck, surrounded by people, comes into view. Children are clinging to the tray or jumping up and down beside the wheels. Mary Pilbara and *no name* Smith's wives, Wilga and Honey, come running from their camps. Wilga is carrying Honey's fat little baby. The older men, Simon Pepper in a white shirt, Lucas Gibson and Ernie Pilbara are walking towards the truck. They are the spokesmen for the community, strong in the law. All three of them were born close to Myrrlumbing; all three have worked on cattle stations or along the coast. They worked for rations and old clothes until citizenship in '67 and after that for wages. All three, Lloyd guesses, have known bad times, on the grog or in whitefeller gaols. They don't like to speak of these things.

One time Simon Pepper did talk about himself. Driving into town in the Landcruiser with Lloyd, he pointed out a spot in the river bed where whitefellers caught him when he was a little feller and sent him away to the Holy Fathers. He didn't learn nothin' there, he said; just cryin' all the time. Pray to your father in heaven, the Holy Fathers told everybody, so one day he give it a try — and that night his own father came sneakin' in and grabbed him out of that place and they ran long, long way right back to the desert.

How little I know about it all, Lloyd thinks. I don't even know their real names, only the names they use for whitefeller forms.

Grabbing his hat with one hand, with the other he shakes tea-leaves into the strainer, pours hot water through them and gulps the drink down. Unloading has started by the time he reaches the truck. Marshall, the drivers and the younger men are carrying sacks and boxes into the store. The women are taking meat and fresh fruit and vegetables from a huge esky. Simon Pepper has lined the children up and is handing out oranges. Lloyd's mouth waters.

"G'day, Lloyd. There's a heap of letters in the cabin."

"Beauty, Mick. How're things?"

Mick, burned as red as the countryside, is one of their usual drivers. The other driver, talking to Ernie Pilbara, hasn't done this run before.

"I'm Lloyd. G'day. Good trip, was it?"

"G'day, mate. Bob, Left Hand Bob, they call me. Yeah, once we got going. There's a pile of letters for you in a box. Picked them up at the Land Council."

"Thanks, mate."

"You want one, Lloyd? You want one?" A girl called Magda is holding out an orange each to Lloyd and Bob though it is Bob she is really talking to, Lloyd realises as they take the oranges. Magda looks strangers right in the face in the whitefellers' bold way. She ran away from some whitefeller up north and got into big trouble in town. The Land Council heard she had relations out at Myrrlumbing and let them know. The relations found her hanging around the pubs, sick and beaten up. She is better now but is restless at Myrrlumbing, fighting with the other women, scheming to get back to the coast.

Ernie Pilbara says something sharply in language, and the girl walks away, her hips sulky.

Lloyd assists with the unloading for half an hour, then looks at his watch. It's time to answer the roll call from the radio base in town. "Would you do the sked this morning, Ernie? I want to take a quick look through the letters before the truck goes back."

"*Yu*." Ernie Pilbara, Lucas Gibson and two or three of the young men go off to the radio in the other Portacom.

"Maybe that letter come today, Lloyd." Mary Pilbara, clutching soap, hair shampoo, carrots and a hand of bananas, sounds hopeful.

"God, I hope so, Mary."

"You sure try hard enough."

He laughs at himself. Of course she doesn't mean his letter from Glencoe, but a letter from Social Security confirming her back pension.

Taking the box of mail from the cabin of the truck, he says to Simon Pepper, the community chairman, "I'll go through all this now — there might be a couple of cheques for you to sign before the truck leaves, Simon, if any bills look urgent."

Marshall's tattoos ripple as he lifts a sack of pumpkins. Tigers snarl, torsos dimple. "Jesus, what are you Lloyd, a bloody bureaucrat?"

Typical Marshall. Always needling other whitefellers. Usually Lloyd doesn't bite. This morning he says "It's what I'm paid to do, you dickhead."

"Yeah, yeah, one of the Department's 'measurable outcomes', is that it?" Marshall walks past him for another load. "That's the way you fellers think, isn't it?"

"You just can't forget I once worked in the public service, can you, Marshall?"

"Did you, Lloyd? Did you really? Mate, I'm not talkin' about your hang-ups, I'm talkin' about the here and now, I'm talkin' about gettin' a side of beef out of the sun!"

Lloyd pursues him, puts his arm across the box Marshall is about to pick up. "Listen, you know what the books were like when I got here." Bloody Marshall. Any moment now he'll have Lloyd saying things like it's public money we're handling, we are accountable — just like any collar-and-tie bunny in some air-conditioned office.

Marshall picks up the box. "Listen matey, what is important about a place like Myrrlumbing — and if you haven't worked this out by now then you better hotfoot it back east damn' smart — is that a group of dispossessed people have come home. Now there's a measurable outcome for you, Lloydie."

"Don't Lloydie me, you prick!"

Of course Marshall is right. People who were born out here, who maybe spent the first ten or twenty years of their lives without seeing a whitefeller, people who fret in towns for their law and their language — these people have come home. That is what matters. On the other hand, as Lloyd is well aware, and so is Marshall — so are the Myrrlumbing people — home has changed. Now they are trespassing in a whitefeller national park. There's not enough bush tucker to go around any more, hence the food truck — and a coordinator knowledgeable enough in whitefeller ways to track down grants and pensions. They all know that plenty of people back there would like to see the collapse of places like Myrrlumbing, the outstations, "settle down country"; would like to see the blackfellers drift back to the towns, whitefellers like Lloyd take to the booze, fiddle the books, chase after the women, plunge screaming mad across the raw dunes.

"Are you listening, Marshall?" Lloyd shouts.

Simon Pepper glances away as Lloyd catches his eye. They don't like the whitefellers quarrelling.

Lloyd flings away. Trudging back to his camp, he flicks through the envelopes, drops the box, gives up looking until he is in the office.

The people have already taken their letters. In the shelter of a clump of tamarugos, Mary Pilbara is reading out a postcard to a group of women. "From Port Moresby," she tells Lloyd. "Long way, eh." It is from the wife of one of Lloyd's predecessors, the guy whose idea it was to plant the tamarugo trees. I'm going to cut the bloody stuff out before I leave, Lloyd tells himself. Salt wattle he likes. Salt wattle grows naturally around the springs, but tamarugo is an exotic from South America. The guy got a grant from the government to plant up the dunes around Myrrlumbing with tamarugo seedlings and to set out hundreds of metres of irrigation hose. He had a grand scheme. The books he left behind in the office are testimony to that: *Dry Land Farming; Salt Tolerant Species; Making the Desert Bloom; Fodder for Stock in Arid Lands*. What stock? Camels? From the top of the dune behind his camp Lloyd sees them in the distance sometimes, around sunset, walking in single file to drink at a spring.

One time when the truck couldn't get through because of a tropical cyclone wandering south and everyone ran short of food, Lucas Gibson shot a camel.

The people at Myrrlumbing don't like shooting camels. "Desert fellers," they tell Lloyd. "Tough. Like us."

Lloyd doesn't have a grand scheme. Just the day-to-day business of doing the sked, doing the paperwork, fixing a tap, replacing a fan belt, deciding whether to call in the flying doctor for a child with a temperature.

He doesn't take weekends off. The people don't — why should he? Anyway, where could he go? It's a day and a half's drive to Glencoe.

Maybe he should have some grand scheme. Something big to get stuck into, see through to the finish.

Her letter has come.

". . . job's great," he skims. "Air-conditioned cabin, power steering. I feel like an ant in charge of an elephant. Got paid again this week. Great place to save if you're not into drinking. Every three months we have to take a long weekend away from Glencoe. Lots of people fly to Darwin then Bali. How does that grab you? I know I've made the right decision, Lloyd darling, even if no one else can understand it except ourselves —"

He reads no further. Tossing the letter aside, he sets about opening envelopes, sorting the contents into stacks on the folding table: cheques to pay in; bills to pay out; replies from the Department; further queries. If there's another bloody request for more information about Mary Pilbara . . . some minor point, trivial, something already covered in his carefully presented arguments for payment of back pay. He's worked hard over Mary Pilbara. All that correspondence backwards and forwards, and the calls over the radio. "Mary Pilbara has been living continuously at Myrrlumbing . . . is the spouse of an invalid pensioner . . . has received no financial assistance . . ." They can't be bloody-minded forever.

There is no letter concerning Mary Pilbara.

Tears rasp his eyelids. Those fuckwits in their cushy of-fices! What more do they want? He scrubs at his eyes, then because his shirt is sticking to him leans away from the back of the chair and wipes his forehead with his arm. His skin feels gritty. With one finger he doodles in the fine red sand covering the table. It turns into a lake with a couple of branching trees, or a heatstruck bird with its feet stretched out. In cities they will be sitting in cool offices, the air-conditioning turned up so high they have to put on jumpers or get out a radiator. In cities they will be dashing off to the cafeteria or the pub. He imagines the sour, chill taste of an ice-cold beer. Here at Myrrlumbing there is no alcohol. Simon Pepper made that clear at Lloyd's inter-view. "No alcohol," Simon told him. "And no mis-sionaries."

He wonders if the drivers have got an esky full of cans stashed away to drink as soon as they are well out on the road.

He could make a cup of tea. He looks up, half-expecting

to see someone standing in the office doorway. He still finds that disconcerting, the way they have of just *being there*. It might be one of the kids, or a young man, or Ernie Pilbara with Mary. If they haven't come for a particular purpose, the older men to talk business, someone to browse through a magazine, old near-blind Esther for a stick of chewing tobacco which she likes to keep in Lloyd's camp, so far to walk it last long time that way, she jokes — if they have come just to watch, Lloyd says hello and goes on with the paperwork, and when he looks up again the person might have disappeared as silently as they came.

There is no one there now. The prickle of irritation he was about to feel turns to disappointment. They could have had a cup of tea together. He can't be bothered lighting the gas ring just for one cup of tea.

He can't be bothered eating, either. Everything he chews feels as though it's been mixed with poppy seed, like those rich chocolate cakes his mother makes whenever he goes home. He sees the white dinner plates on her yellow tablecloth, crisp green salads, drops pearling down the side of a chilled glass.

Maybe he's the wrong person for the job. Maybe he should chuck it all in right now — hitch back to town with the truck. Maybe his old man was right. He's a drifter. Can't stick at anything. Clerk; gardener; brickie's labourer; taxi driver; clerk again. All useful for his present job, they commented at the interview. Yeah? He should have stayed put that first time, eight-thirty to four-fifty-one till the day he carked it.

He could disappear into the dunes.

Putting his chair across the piles of letters to stop them blowing about, he goes outside. He looks around cautiously. Dexter gives him a wave from the other side of the lake. Ignoring the dust, he is wheeling an old bicycle down to Lake Alba to ride around on the crusty salt. Lloyd waves back, and pretends he is on the way to the tap. At his approach a pair of black and white wagtails fly up into the tamarugos, chittering and darting their tails. He drinks sparingly, then rinses his mouth. The water is fresh and sweet, with a cold mineral taste.

Maybe the drivers would sling him a few cans on the quiet. Drink them in the middle of the night — who would know?

From one of the camps a woman appears and makes her way towards the rocky end of the dune. It is the place the women like to use. He's had a pit toilet dug but they prefer the open air.

He realises he is staring and turns away.

Close to the settlement, lengths of black irrigation hose lie rotting in the sun. That's one thing about the sun, thinks Lloyd, it wears away everything in time, shit and schemes alike.

He sees a man in a white shirt coming towards him from the store. Simon Pepper. Lloyd's heart gives him a thump in the neck. Nothing escapes Simon Pepper.

Waiting for him, trapped in flight, he wonders if Simon's white shirts in this climate are a small vanity. Simon Pepper is an imposing-looking man. Very black, very thin, with greying hair and cicatrices on his chest, he walks swiftly; you would never guess how bad his sight is, the result of years of trachoma and cataracts. Now his attention is caught by something on the sand. He picks up a piece of paper and examines it closely, then puts it in his shirt pocket.

Lloyd makes an effort. "Ready to go back to town, are they, Simon?"

"Soon. Havin' something to eat first in Ernie Pilbara's camp. One of them fellers cousin to Ernie Pilbara. Livin' on the coast now, drivin' trucks. Haven't seen Ernie for years."

"Left Hand Bob?"

"*Yu.*"

"Maybe he wants to come and live out here at Myrrlumbing."

"Maybe."

"He'd be good at looking after the vehicles."

"Maybe."

Lloyd is surprised at Simon's lack of enthusiasm for a relation. Simon is the one who gathers his people together. If he takes eighty people to a funeral at Alice, eighty-five come back.

"Maybe you've heard things about him, Simon?"

Simon Pepper shrugs. "Good bloke, I reckon. *Yu.* Good bloke."

"Hits the grog, maybe?"

Simon shrugs again, and Lloyd's stomach churns: he has gone too far with his whitefeller questioning. Jesus, when will he learn! "How about a cup of tea?" he says hastily. "I've been through the mail. There are a couple of bills we should pay rightaway. I've made out the cheques. They're in there ready for you to sign."

While Lloyd lights the gas ring, Simon goes into the office and puts on his glasses. Lloyd can't help glancing at him. After he has looked over the letters he places a pen carefully between thumb and forefinger. His body grows tense with concentration. He's just great, thinks Lloyd. Able to read the desert since childhood, he learned whitefeller writing barely twelve months ago. Years ago — maybe it was in gaol — it came to him to find his people and bring them home. There would be the law and there would be a bilingual school. One morning last summer, casting aside his memories of that bad time with the Holy Fathers, he walked into the schoolroom and, sitting down with the children and the younger adults, said "I need learning."

Lloyd smiles at the unintended ironies in that statement.

He mixes powdered milk in a cup. "Tea's ready when you are, Simon."

He makes sure Simon's tea is how he likes it, lukewarm with plenty of milk and sugar. They sit in the doorway to drink it. Simon Pepper sits quietly, Lloyd searches for something to say, to drop like sugar into the milky silence.

"I reckon we should chop out those tamarugos. Salt wattles are fine, they've always been here, but not those bloody tamarugos." As Simon says nothing, just turns his head towards the tamarugos where several women are resting in their shade, Lloyd continues "They don't come from this part of the world. Some silly bugger introduced them."

Simon Pepper sips his tea.

"They're from another country," adds Lloyd.

Simon says nothing.

Another irony strikes Lloyd. "Okay — same as whitefellers," he says.

They both laugh.

A woman walks from her camp to a tap under the salt wattles. It is Magda, who ran away from her people and got into trouble in town.

Simon Pepper says "Maybe Rhyll come back soon."

"I hope so. She's still driving trucks at Glencoe."

"Bad place, that Glencoe. All our sacred place there dug up."

"That's for sure."

"She done good job with the books."

"Sure. Quicker than me." But it isn't *my* job, is it? she said one evening. I don't have a place here, not a real place, Lloyd. They had their second argument then. He frowns, watching Magda walk back to her relations' camp.

Simon says "Whitefellers driftin' round by themselves, I seen plenty up north. No good. You get Rhyll to come back. You tell her the people here like that. Eh?"

Lloyd laughs. Simon sounds like his parents and Rhyll's, except that they say Couldn't you two find more comfortable jobs together on the coast? "I'll tell her, Simon."

"Maybe your parents come for a visit."

"Here?" The people don't want visitors, Lloyd has come to understand — whitefellers poking about, asking a lot of silly questions, taking photographs and putting them in books — the people don't want that; they want to be left alone, get on with their living.

"*Yu.*"

"I reckon my parents would like that very much."

"Maybe when it's cooler, eh. You tell them."

He certainly will. He'll call them up on the radio this afternoon. This is your son, over . . . I'm fine, over . . . I've got a special invitation for you, what about coming over? Over.

Simon feels in his shirt pocket. "I picked this up. You must've dropped it."

It is another letter from some department. Lloyd opens it, then reads avidly. "Listen to this — they've agreed to pay Mary Pilbara's back pension!"

"Bout time, eh."

He passes the letter to Simon. When Simon has finished looking at it he says "Good. Real good, Lloyd. Maybe we try for that new airstrip now."

"I was thinking the very same thing." He refills their cups. "That airstrip ought to be our next project. Yes. It most certainly should. I'll start phoning up right away, I'll drive into town — I'll go all the way to Canberra if I have to!"

"You tell them fellers, Lloyd!"

*   *   *

"This is a good place, Lloyd, I reckon."

They sit looking out over the settlement. The wind must have eased; Lloyd can see almost to the other end of Lake Alba. In the lake bed Dexter is riding in figures of eight. Half a dozen children are chasing him. A dog barks. They are all male dogs here: a community decision. Under the tamarugos a woman is washing clothes in a tub and hanging them on the branches to dry. One of Ernie Pilbara's boys is carrying home four huge cabbages. He drops them, and a child pounces on one and runs off with it, laughing.

"*Yu*, Simon. This is a good place."

CAPITAL GAINS

Pray silence for the Speaker

One of the kids should be clearing the table. Joan Skerritt is on the point of asking whose turn it is when on to the screen comes that commentator who gabs on about money, the funny one, Mr Earnest himself, and Joan starts laughing before he has opened his mouth. " — additional costs," he hisses, lifting his chin at her. He's talking about Canberra, but you can't help watching him. His glasses and his bald head gleam. As usual, he's standing in front of the long white building with the twin rows of flagpoles. Knitting needles, Joan thinks, and wonders if it's too late this winter to start another jumper for one of the kids. Slowly Mr Earnest half-closes his eyes. Joan glances around the table. Trish and Lurlene are grinning — even Alvie is taken in. Young Billy's cradling his cup just like his father. The camera zooms in for a close-up. Mr Earnest is going to jump right in to their living room. " — revised estimates," he whispers with a tiny nod, pausing unblinking to let the words sink in.

Any moment now Ray Skerritt will say "What did I tell you?" He actually listens to all this stuff. To everyone's surprise he reaches across and reduces the man to a mouthing, gesturing mute. (He's even funnier when you can't hear the words.)

"Move your elbows, Billy, Lurlene," says Ray Skerritt. "Make a bit of room there." Over the table he spreads a map of south-eastern Australia. "Canberra," he says, tapping with a blunt fingertip. "Canberra. I was thinking it's about time these kids saw a bit of their national capital, Joan."

"Canberra! That's a turnaround," the oldest girl Alvie scoffs. "You're always knocking the place. You're the original Canberra knocker. The fat cats. The silk department. The last outpost of Empire. Now you want to go there."

"And why not?" says Ray Skerritt with the excessive cheerfulness he's taken to using with Alvie since she's come back to Hazelwood. "Take a gander for ourselves. See where our money goes. And another thing — next time I run into old Poddy Bull, I'll be able to have a proper go at him. Eh Trish?"

Trish, a placid-looking girl in her mid-teens, looks at her father admiringly. He's not scared to say what he thinks. He's always getting into arguments with people, even the guys he works with, even the ones who voted him shop steward. He's against uranium. He says you can't vote for someone just because he might put a few more dollars in your pocket. When the company invited Mr Bull, MP, to tour the paper mill just before the '84 election, and Mr Bull said he'd like to have lunch with the workers in the newly-built canteen that union men like Ray Skerritt had pushed for for years, her father found himself sitting opposite Mr Bull. And when everyone was being polite because it was a visitor for lunch not an election rally, Ray Skerritt leaned across the table and said right to Mr Bull's face, "Better watch it this time, Poddy! This time the writing's in the tea-leaves for sure."

When Ray Skerritt got off the mill bus that afternoon he was still laughing.

Joan Skerritt is thinking *Canberra*, so that's what he's had on his mind, is it? She thinks But it's such a cold place! She thinks Though I could get a good bit of knitting done in the car. She smiles down at the teapot. Canberra — isn't Canberra where Richard Potter is, gorgeous Chainsaw Potter from high school whom she ran into in Melbourne a couple of Christmases ago? Gorgeous dreamboat Chainsaw . . . she was only in second form and he was the new boy in fifth. He wrote that gruesome murder play that was put on at speech night, and everyone's parents said when they recovered from all the blood they just knew one day he'd put the school, the town, the nation on the map! "Excuse me," this stooped, greying man with the briefcase startled her as she was about to cross Collins Street, "Joan — it couldn't be, yes it is — Joan Lafferty!" "Chainsaw Potter!" Christmas shoppers surged around them as they swapped condensed histories until, glancing up, Chainsaw Potter exclaimed "Here's my tram, Joan, I'll have to run, I've got a meeting at the top of town." Swinging out over the step he shouted "Joan if ever you're in Canberra give me a ring at the office — not in the phone book — have you out for a meal. Don't forget!"

Joan hasn't told the family about this chance meeting. She intended to, of course, in the car on the way home from the Hazelwood station, or later, her shoes slipped off and her feet up on the sofa, Guess what happened to me in Collins Street today? but the words stayed unspoken. She couldn't say why, exactly. Perhaps she was interrupted — Ray telling her about something out at the mill, or the kids carrying on about what she had in the parcels.

Perhaps she hung back from peering too closely: peachy Chainsaw in Collins Street had such a shabby briefcase.

"Canberra's a long way from anywhere," she says carefully, testing.

"Rubbish!" Ray responds, tapping the map with his

knuckle. "Look. We go through Lakes Entrance to Orbost and from Orbost to Cann River —"

"Better get the diff fixed if you want to get further than Sale, Dad," Billy says.

"What? Yes all right, Billy. Are you listening to this? Orbost to Cann River, then up the Cann Valley Highway —"

The lovely names run like a litany through Trish's head . . . Noorinbee. Bombala. Nimmitabel. Cooma. "Ha!" her father is laughing. "Poddy Hut! Here's a place called Poddy Hut. If you people could be packed up and ready first thing, we'd make Canberra in a day. Easy. I was thinking the next school break, Joan, what do you reckon?"

"That's fixed then: the next school break everyone goes to Canberra," Alvie Skerritt pronounces before her mother can speak. Pulling a magazine at random from the rack, she adds "You can count me out."

"Oh good, there'll be more room in the car," Lurlene says.

Trish sees her parents glance at Alvie and then at each other. What now? the glances plead. Her round pink face grows pinker. "Do come, Alv," she says for them. "Do come and have fun with your family."

"Why?" says Alvie.

"Canberra's much colder than here, Trish," Joan Skerritt says promptly, as though Canberra's cold could be the only possible explanation for Alvie's reluctance — Alvie who, when Philip Jennaway came back to Australia, chose to stay on alone through winter in Oxford, with blizzards in Europe night after night on the Skerritts' TV, and icicles forming on the inside of her window.

"You can borrow my coat, Trish," Alvie offers suddenly. "You can keep it if you want."

"Your coloured coat? Your lovely coloured coat that Philip gave you? You're giving your coat away?" Lurlene claps her hand over her mouth because in Alvie's hearing she has slipped and said *that name*.

"You better get that diff fixed, Dad," Billy says.

That is how, when the Skerritts set out for Canberra at the end of one cold, sunny August — Joan, Ray, Trish, Billy and Lurlene — Lurlene, between Billy and Trish, is on the lookout for weddings; Billy is wondering if they'll let him drive for a bit on some out-of-the-way stretch through the mountains; Ray is thinking it's a shame they've just missed Parliament in session, he'd love to see Hawkie making mincemeat of old Poddy; Joan is trying to remember which department Richard Potter said he worked in; and Trish is wearing Alvie's coat. She keeps stroking it. The material is cotton, with a silky finish that she finds luxurious. Alvie and Philip bought it at a special place in London, so Alvie wrote to the Skerritts. "I feel so happy when I'm wearing it," she scrawled on one of her infrequent postcards, and no wonder! With its crimson diamonds on creamy-white and its great bold borders of purple, sea-green, peacock-blue and gold, you couldn't keep your eyes off it as it swung from her shoulders that morning at Tullamarine as she came through customs, waving to her family then looking eagerly around the crowd, searching . . .

In another place

Through the field the road runs by To many-towered Camelot runs the poem through Trish's head as the world flies past — trees, farms, little towns, trucks loaded with logs or cattle or shining car bodies.

Her parents are taking turns to drive — at least, that is what Ray Skerritt says they will do, although when her mother murmurs "Do you want a break now, dear?" Ray replies cheerfully "She's apples for a bit longer," and Joan doesn't insist.

With colours gay — with colours gay Trish perseveres. A stupid poem, Alvie's voice breaks in. An utterly puerile, pathetic, piss-weak poem, why do you go for that stuff Trish, Tennyson's just a typical overbearing male who has to do in any female who tries to stand up for herself.

Sometimes Trish astonishes herself. "I know what's wrong with you!" she shouted at Alvie one afternoon as she scooped up her sister's dirty knickers and a shirt freshly ironed by their mother and a purse and the dogeared diary Alvie leaves lying around knowing Trish never looks, she just wouldn't; Lurlene on the other hand's a real little sticky, or even their mother, thinking about something else, might flip through it, starting at the last page the way she reads books.

Trish flung everything across the room on to Alvie's bed.

"And what is wrong with me?" said Alvie, very quietly, picking up the diary.

"*She hath no loyal knight and true,*" minced Trish.

Alvie said nothing to that, just turned away to the small drawer on her side of the dressing-table. Tipping out a hoard of hair pins, combs, pieces of hat elastic, odd earrings, she scrabbled amongst them until she found the key, never used, to all the drawers. "You just don't have a clue, do you?" she said at last, putting the diary in the empty drawer. With a tiny triumphant smile at Trish she turned the key in the lock.

Lurlene traces one finger over the stitching of Alvie's coat. "It's lovely, Trish, I wish it was mine," she says, cuddling against her sister and gazing up into her face. "You're lucky, Trish. Aren't you lucky?"

"What are you whispering for?" Trish says, twitching away.

They stay overnight after all, at Bombala. In the morning, as Ray Skerritt scrapes crystals of frost off the windscreen and back window of the car, the others stand clapping their gloved hands and taking in the sharp, glassy air as though it is a portent of Canberra.

In spite of the frost, one by one they strip off gloves and scarves in the car as the sun pours over them. Beyond Cooma, car after car flying towards them has bundles of skis tied to the roof-rack. "Lucky pigs," Billy grumbles, craning to watch as they disappear into the distance.

"Come on, you're doing all right." Frowning into the rear-vision mirror at the receding skiers, Ray Skerritt adds, "Out of the pockets of the likes of us, Joannie."

"Slow *down*, Ray," Joan says.

It is midmorning before Ray Skerritt tells them they are nearing the border. The blue sky glitters, the car flies uphill over a wide smooth road. The railway line running parallel draws them on. As it crosses a high wooden bridge, Ray Skerritt ducks his head at a road sign and declares "There you are, folks, there she is! Did you see what that sign said? Canberra thirty-five kil*ome*tres."

"The border? Is that *all*?" says Lurlene.

"*Kil*-o-metres," says Trish.

Her father's hands lift off the steering wheel and drop back.

*   *   *

Along the railway line, roadside hoardings spring up like
strange trees promising their fruits in the approaching city.
The road becomes narrower, rougher. Stony paddocks,
unlike the lush green dairy farms they are used to around
Hazelwood, seem to them full of nothing but tussocks and
thistles and briars.

Billy points out a solitary patch of snow under a rocky
outcrop.

I wonder how Alvie's getting on all on her own, Ray
Skerritt ponders.

I don't *care*, Trish tells herself fiercely. It's her fault, it
has to be, *he's* just the same as he always was.

Lurlene is counting farmhouses now. Billy's teasing her
again. "You can't have that one. You can't even see it for
all the oak trees."

Ray, glancing, imagines some pale English settler thrust
in to this freeze-dried landscape. Poor bugger, Ray thinks,
he had to plant English trees, couldn't bring himself to
look out on his new country. "It's a hard bloody country,"
he says, "for a nation's capital."

They pass tussocky flats running down to a creek. Trish,
catching sight of a family of saplings clustered around an
old gnarled gum tree, thinks It isn't right! She should have
come!

What Ray sees is one huge eucalypt standing head and
shoulders above the rest. Gorbachev, he thinks. Whitlam.
Waiting their chance to do him in, he broods, looking at
the smaller trees circling, pressing in. He laughs silently.
That's what they do to you in this hard bloody life.

Joan breaks across reveries. "My God, those peaks!" she
says. "Stop for a minute, Ray."

They get out of the car, stretching and grumbling, then
fall into silence as a rush of valleys sweeps them up to
mountains brilliant in the midday light. Coree, Ginini,

Gingera, Bimberi, says Trish hastily, the names a talisman. Behind the mountains, what hidden peaks and gullies, what further parts of the range lie out of sight, like something never truly known? She shivers, and turns back to the car. "Can I sit next to you, Mum?" she wants to ask, but says instead "Swap seats, Dad? I'm getting stiff," and "Why don't you let Mum drive, Dad?" so that Ray Skerritt, climbing into the back, thinks She's getting like Alvie, our little Trish, Trish was always the easy one, not like Alv, what happens to these girls?

Point of order

Unexpectedly, they catch their first glimpses of the city. On their left, imposing order on a straggly hillside, are newly-constructed crescents and circuits and avenues, then rows of new brown brick houses, and a woman in a crimson headscarf pegging out a line of napkins. On their right on a distant mountain top a hypodermic plunges into the taut skin of the sky.

The road turns, and the tower stands straight in front of them, a beacon. Not far now to the city. They all sit up, smooth their clothes, touch their hair. Their mouths get ready to say the things people say coming into Canberra: What wide streets! Isn't it clean! Isn't it pretty! Everything laid on! Nobody walking! Such clear air! So clean and neat!

From the back of a truck a roadside hawker is selling bunches of daffodils bright as egg yolks. Lurlene says she's starving. "We'll be seeing embassies soon," her father tells her. "Try counting flags, why don't you?"

At last they are on a wide street where plane trees are coming into leaf. They peer eagerly, and see stolid red brick houses with red tiles and white window frames looking out on to yellowed, frostbitten grass. Not a flag in sight. Trucks rush past them: a load of pine logs; a truckful of sheep; a concrete mixer painted harsh pink. They are suddenly quiet. Is *this* Canberra, houses no bigger than the doctor's in Hazelwood, sheep like sale day, logs like any mill town? Ray Skerritt, looking ahead, sees a red flag fluttering above a tall bluish-green hedge; he opens his mouth then closes it, falling like the others into a broody silence.

And then, as they come uphill to traffic lights, filling their windscreen are the rising walls of a huge building, the immense area it covers scaling down its height so that confronting them it appears comprehensible, graspable, biddable even, its dozens of great windows narrowing to the slits of Trish's medieval tower. Over it bend seven white and red cranes, their cables no more than threads of cotton binding the ice-blue sky.

Lurlene, counting, is the first to say something. "Seven ladies with bustles!"

"Pollies pigging at a trough."

"What are you on about, Billy?" his father exclaims, straining forward against his seat belt. "That's it, the new Parliament House, that's why the whole shebang's here —" He gestures widely. "All this — Canberra!"

"— where our money goes," Billy adds, confident as an echo.

"Well you don't expect to get a national symbol for nothing, do you!" his father retorts.

Question without notice

Glancing in the rear vision mirror, Joan slows to a crawl around State Circle so that they can take in the activity on Capital Hill. They see enormous front-end loaders pouring earth over a new bank; stacks of what look like giant baby's baths; builders' sheds; tiny figures in hard hats; shrubs and trees springing back in planned sections.

"Go right round again, Joannie," Ray Skerritt says as they come to the turn-off to the city. "We've got our two bob in all this, too."

"Check out that wall, will ya!" Billy sighs. "Gimme a can of spray paint."

Ray Skerritt chuckles. "Someone's beaten you to it, son."

A minute figure on a ladder is at work restoring the wall's pristine surface. The graffiti stretches ahead of him. In huge red letters they read CELEBRATE IN 88.

"Why is the circle of that eight a face crying?" Lurlene asks. "Oh pooh, he's scrubbed out the rest."

Trish cranes behind her mother. "Not quite — you can make something out."

"I get it!" Billy shouts. "See? WHITE AUSTRALIA HAS A BLACK HISTORY DON'T — "

"They've got a job cleaning that off," Joan says.

"It'll be back again tomorrow," says Ray Skerritt.

Madam Speaker

"Toot! Toot!" says Trish suddenly. Stretching across her mother's arm, she jabs at the horn as they pass a brightly painted shack with a rough sign at the front. Amongst tussocks and daisies it squats like a poor relation at the gates of an imposing brick building.

As her mother says "Barley, Charlie! Hands off!" Trish, aghast at her own urgency, hears herself rushing on "But didn't you see the sign? That's the Liberation Centre outside the South African Embassy and they want everyone to toot if they're against apartheid! We are, aren't we? Well we *are*, aren't we?"

"Since when have you been a political activist?" Billy smirks as she peers back for a last look.

Her father says "No need to demonstrate our solidarity by getting us killed," and Billy has to add as they come to the lake's edge and turn under a bridge, "Now look what you've done, you've made Mum miss Commonwealth Avenue."

Trish's face burns. She hears her mother say "No worries, boys. Just thought we'd take a quick look over this way."

Well, I'm bushed good and proper now, Joan thinks. Isn't this what they say about Canberra? Round and round in circles. Like my life, she adds, struck by the idea. She glances at Trish and then in the mirror at the others. Alvie has stepped off. Or thinks she has. Why not me, too? And Joan feels a pinch of anticipation, subtle as salt. Follow my nose, she tells herself.

The curving road takes her past rose gardens and fountains and the long white building with the twin rows of flagpoles. "Parliament," says Ray Skerritt, watching a policeman walk up the wide steps, and thinking So that's where Whitlam stood ten years ago, head and shoulders above everyone else while some clown proclaimed his overthrow. He hears a voice, Alvie's, piping *Oh how the mighty are fallen!* — something smart she picked up from Philip, doubtless. He stares at the National Gallery and at the

High Court whose bold chunky angles and shadows he tells himself reflect the vision of that man, that giant deposed by pygmies. *Go Ahead!* That was one of Whitlam's election slogans. What a fool Ray was at the time not to have got hold of a few spare dollars somehow, run up debts, pleaded with the bank for an overdraft, gone to a moneylender — anything — in order to get to Canberra before Malcolm Fraser and his schemers on the Opposition benches gave Gough Whitlam the chop.

Now he'll have to be content with looking at Whitlam's portrait amongst all the other ex-prime ministers in King's Hall. They say it's an unusual painting, modern, not formal like most of them. They say you used to see Whitlam walking to work just like anybody else, striding high between the Lodge and Parliament House. Ray stares out at people eating lunch in the bright wintry sunshine. He stares at the fountain soaring from the lake and falling back on itself in a sheet of blown drops. Vivid as a rainbow a small fantasy forms inside his head. He's driving, not Joan; he's passing a traffic island and guess who's standing on it waiting for a break in the traffic? Ray slows to a stop, winds down the window. "Go ahead!" he says, waving the big man forward as traffic banks up behind them. "Go ahead!" says Ray to Gough Whitlam.

Joggers are everywhere. In shorts and singlets they pursue one another doggedly across the bridge, around the lake's edge, along the grassy kerb-sides. Suddenly one of them, a man with red, rapt face, charges across the road in front of the car so that Joan has to slam on the brakes.

"Toot the idiot!" Ray says.

Hearing the horn, the man turns and mouths something. His stride doesn't falter.

"Close encounters of the Canberran kind," breathes Billy.

There's another jogger standing at the edge of the road while several cars pass. When Joan comes level she stops.

"Go on!" Ray says impatiently. "You've got right of way," but Joan waves the jogger across. "She'd been standing there for ages," she says.

"Female solidarity, Dad," Trish says, and Joan laughs.

"You're getting to sound just like Alvie, the way you talk sometimes," Ray Skerritt grumbles.

"It's because she's wearing Alvie's coat," Lurlene says.

The Honourable Member will resume his seat

The first thing Ray sees as he walks up the steps into King's Hall is the chin of the man who plotted the king hit. The chin lifts arrogantly from the canvas; the blue eyes stare, the mouth tilts in faint derision.

The bastard! Ray says to himself. The bastard! Not even Whitlam close by can dissipate the old anger. Ray searches his portrait for a fitting sense of bigness, but is unable to find it. The eyes are right: intense, far-reaching, but the face seems too small for them, as though the artist had in mind the wasting of the man, the reduction.

"Come on, Ray," Joan says. "The guide's ready."

Because Parliament is in recess just now, the chambers empty, the politicians dispersed, visitors are taken on a tour. The guide leads them up the narrow winding stairs into the public gallery of the House of Representatives.

"Go right down to the front," Ray Skerritt tells them. "Billy! Down here. Don't lean over the balcony, Lurlene, can't you read the sign? You can't knit in here, Joan. Joan —"

"Keep your wool on, dear."

"Shh! He wants to get started, Joan."

"Here in this chamber we have what is truly the people's house," the guide tells them. "You'll notice that all the furnishings are green — carpet, upholstery, telephone — after the House of Commons, the mother of parliaments on which so many of our parliamentary procedures are based, not least our cherished freedom of speech — "

The guide's voice grows fainter. On the floor of the House, Ray sees the double doors swing open and the members crowd in. There's a sense of urgency this afternoon; they take their seats quickly, murmur briefly.

At the central green table Whitlam and Fraser are seated opposite each other. Prime Minister and Leader of the Opposition. The member for Wirrawa and the member for Wannon. They have been arm-wrestling for weeks. Neither can budge the other. Hang on a bit longer, Ray wills Gough, he'll crack, he'll back off, he'll come to see it's what the people want, it's what they chose.

Pray silence for the Speaker —

There's a hush so glassy you could cut yourself.

I call the Honourable Member for Wannon —

Mr Speaker, this afternoon the Governor-General commissioned me to form a government —

Before he can get out another word Ray Skerritt is on his feet, leaning right out over the railing, shouting "Sit down, Fraser! Shame! Shame! Gough, we want Gough!" *Gough! Gough!* — the cry is taken up around the crowded, straining gallery, it rings through the solid walls, it is echoed by anxious people rushing upon Parliament House, filling King's Hall, spilling over the steps and into the courtyard, trampling the rose gardens, pouring across the city's bridges from the surrounding towns and the farms, rallying across the nation: *We want Gough!*

Startled faces look up from the floor of the House, Malcolm Fraser is scowling, Gough Whitlam acknowledges Ray with a boxer's salute.

An attendant in green rushes at Ray. His arm is seized, joggled. "This way, Ray!"

It is only Joan. She is on her feet. "Coming, dear? We're going over to the Senate now."

I name the Honourable Member!

"Where are the politicians?" Lurlene demands as they come back into King's Hall. "I want to see the politicians."

"Not much hope," Ray Skerritt tells her. "They'll be in warmer places than this right now, no worries. Gold Coast, Bali."

As he speaks, a familiar figure appears out of a passageway. Ray Skerritt stares. The man catches his eye; hand outstretched, he hurries towards them across King's Hall. Ray nudges Joan: Poddy Bull!

Poddy Bull is talking before he reaches them. "It's Ray, isn't it? Ray . . . Skerritt, that's right, of course — on the tip of my tongue. Now don't tell me . . . lunch . . . Hazelwood paper mill . . . And this is your family? Joan — Joan, very, very nice to meet you." He shakes hands vigorously, repeating each name as Ray introduces them. "That's a neat coat you've got there!" he says to Trish. "Wouldn't want to do a swap, would you?" "It's my sister's," mumbles Trish. "Yes? And what brings you people to Canberra? Family? Sightseeing? Well, so what do you think of this place, eh? You're right, the new one's much bigger. You should see the office I'm in now, hardly room for the typewriter. To tell you the truth, government backbenchers aren't much better off. Pity there's not an open day at the new House while you're up here. You could have had lamingtons and tea in the PM's suite. Had a good look round, have you? Sorry I can't take you in to lunch, my pleasure, but (looking at his watch) I'm off to —"

"Bali?" Lurlene puts in.

"Bali?" He scratches his neck. "You're a little bit keen on Bali, are you, lassie? It was all British history when your daddy and I were at school. No, I've got one of those weeks coming up. I'm on a committee. We have a lot of our meetings when the House isn't sitting. That's where most of the work gets done, you know, on these parliamentary committees."

"It doesn't sound as though your family gets to see much of you, Mr Bull," Joan comments.

"You're right, Mrs Skerritt, they don't. I'm either up here in Canberra or else as you know I'm out and about looking after my constituents, my word I am! No, it's tough for our families. And next time round, next time round when our blokes are back sitting on the other side of the House, Ray, I'll see even less of them."

"He didn't mean that about taking us to lunch if he wasn't busy, did he, Dad?" Lurlene asks.

Ray Skerritt laughs. "Don't be so ready to disbelieve people . . . Well, fancy running into Poddy Bull! That's a turn-up for the books. Just think of it, Joan, he's meeting new faces all the time, and how long is it since he was out at the mill, how many years? And he remembered who I was!" He chuckles. "I bet he remembers exactly what I said, too! I told him, I said Watch it Poddy! Your number's up! And I was right, wasn't I, well not about him personally, he's a survivor, cunning old coot, but about what people wanted, wanting change, wanting to go forward again. I told him to his face!" Ray Skerritt is still chuckling. "I'll say this for him, though, he keeps his nose down, the old Poddy." They go out the glass doors and, standing on the spot where on Remembrance Day 1975 a bloodless coup was declared, look out across the courtyard, across the quiet lawns and the lake and the great sweeping drive towards the War Memorial. "That's why people go on voting for him," Ray Skerritt is saying. "That's something, that is — remembering a bloke's name like that!"

And your petitioners as in duty bound will ever pray

"Isn't that lucky, Ray!" Joan Skerritt is seated at the mirror in their room at the Grevillea Motor Lodge. She flicks the collar of her new cream blouse, smooths its softness over waist and hips. She's wearing it with her black skirt, her good one. Smart, her reflection tells her, just right for this evening. She smiles back at herself. It's the sort of blouse worn tucked in or out. She's wearing it out; no one will know she lets out her waistbands with a safety pin these days. She holds a pair of large dangling parrots against her ears. "The Potters living in the very next street, I mean," she goes on. "Baynton Street. You don't think these earrings are a bit, a bit *young*, do you, Ray? Isn't it a coincidence? Mrs Potter says they're just around the corner. We can walk there in five minutes." She leans into her reflection and turns her head from side to side. "What do you think, Ray?"

Ray Skerritt, in his navy-blue suit that he bought for somebody's wedding, Joan's sister's it must have been, is holding a red, yellow and blue striped tie in one hand and a green and maroon tie in the other. Looking at his wife at the mirror, he remembers an apricot tree growing against somebody's fence, its fruit bursting with ripeness and its branches a flurry of startled rosellas as he reached in from the street.

"No — no, fine, they'll do," he says.

"Of course they're not too young, Mum! They're just great, Mum! Far out! Ace!" Trish and Lurlene chorus. They are already dressed for going out, and are curled up out of the way on their bunks.

"You girls would insist I buy them!"

Ray Skerritt blinks. The way he remembers it, Joan, in a downstairs jangly shop that caught her eye in Civic Centre this morning, held up one gaudy parrot against Trish's ear and one against Lurlene's, saying "These are just right — aren't these just right?" so that, hanging about waiting halfway down the stairs of that place with its sweet smoky odour and its bored-looking salesgirl with the stud through her nose like a bull on show day, he wasn't sure whether it was Trish or young Lurlene Joan had in mind before she sparkled on "Yes, I'll definitely take these earrings!" And none of them has caught sight of them again until this minute.

"She sounded very nice on the phone," Joan continues. The scarlet and blue birds swing against her neck as she slips the hooks through her ears and flourishes her head. "Mrs Potter. Her name's Angel. What's that short for, d'you think?"

"Search me. This Potter's a collar-and-tie bloke, I suppose." Maybe Joan already knew where Potter lived, just around the corner, five minutes' walk away, when she booked them into the Grevillea back in Hazelwood. Ray scowls at the parrots. He was all for a caravan park until Joan talked him out of it. Said it wouldn't be handy. Handy to what? Fair go, he reminds himself, she had to ring Potter at work to get his address. First thing Monday morning she rang him: Richard Potter? You'll never guess . . . Yes, Canberra! Really and truly Canberra! — and half an hour later his wife was phoning Joan at the Grevillea making an evening for dinner.

"Which do you reckon?" Ray asks, holding out the ties.

The houses in Baynton Street are small, brick, each the mirror image of its neighbour, and set well back behind shin-high fences. "These Canberrans are certainly shy about displaying house numbers," Ray Skerritt comments. Secretive! he says to himself. Arrogant! And as he goes on peering takes a gloomy pleasure in repeating Arrogant! Secretive!

"What does this chap Potter do?" he asks Joan.

"He's in the public service. I told you that, dear. He got married years after most of us, and they've got one little girl."

"I said, what does he *do*?"

Joan doesn't answer. Just because Ray's had to put on a tie! She finds a house number and starts counting. "This must be it," she says doubtfully, stopping in front of a forest of spindly gums and banksias. They make their way to a small porch with firewood stacked against one wall.

As Joan raps on the frosted glass door panel, Lurlene says "This isn't a bit posh, there isn't even a doorbell!" and Ray Skerritt adds "Are you sure you've got the right street, Joan?" "Oh shoosh!" breathes Trish in an agony of embarrassment, convinced someone on the other side of the door, overhearing, will think these Skerritts have never been anywhere.

A stranger in the House

The bloke looks buggered, Ray Skerritt thinks as he shakes hands with Richard Potter. Potter's skin is pale, grey almost, and there are furrows running from his cheekbones to his jaw. Poor bugger looks ten years older than me already, Ray thinks, and gives Potter's hand an extra shake.

"What a splendid coat!" Potter says, hanging their things in the hall. ("It's my sister's," Trish mutters.) "Come in by the fire — come and meet Angel and Emma." He's wearing sports trousers and a polo-neck shirt — no tie; Ray makes up his mind to get rid of his just as soon as he can.

How on earth do blokes like Potter who look about ready for the knackers . . . is Ray's first impression of Mrs Potter. Sitting up very straight on the sofa, she is looking up expectantly, her face, no, her whole person alight, welcoming, her dark hair coiled around her head, one ankle above very high heels crossed over the other, her instep carved like a dancer's, and so smooth it looks sculpted. In a flash Ray Skerritt registers all this, then Mrs Potter has sprung to her feet and, hand outstretched, is coming to greet them.

She's wearing black velvet trousers and a silk shirt — tucked in, Joan notices, pulling in her stomach. Potter's wife has this modern thing of shaking hands, Ray sees; Alvie's picked it up too. "This is Emma," says Mrs Potter, one arm around the shoulders of a small, glowing girl. "And I'm Angel Drimys."

Huh, one of those relationships, is it? Ray Skerritt glances at Potter. Joan's laughing her meeting-new-people laugh. "Drimys. You kept your own name?"

"Her father's," Ray puts in drily.

"No, it's really hers," the child Emma tells them. "She

chose it herself. It's a shrub she likes, mountain pepper."

Trish thinks Angel Drimys, Angel Drimys. She's different, she's got an accent — Spanish is it or something more wonderful — Persian? Malay? And the room's lovely, friendly, with that hot fire, and all the flowers even though it's still winter, creamy-white jonquils you can smell right across the room, and everlastings the colour of summer, and those dried things in an old crock, we could do that at home, and the paintings on the walls, what are those black and gold puppets with the funny faces?

"What can I get you to drink?" Richard Potter asks. Oh dear, thinks Joan, This is Canberra, I mustn't say sweet sherry. "Beer for me," Ray is about to reply when Richard says "Champagne?" and pours for all of them, Trish and Billy too, and a splash with mineral water for Lurlene and Emma, so that Joan thinks So this is how things are done in Canberra! and Ray thinks He's putting on an act for Joan, damned public service!

"This reminds me of that party, Richard," Joan bubbles. "Remember? After your play? He wrote this play for speech night, Angel, full of all these ghastly murders. That's how the name Chainsaw came about —" She pauses. Angel Drimys is smiling as though she isn't quite listening. Richard is uncorking a second bottle. "— terribly funny, really," she continues on indrawn breath. "Everyone fainting, all the parents and the stuffy old councillors, and I had to scream, in the play I mean, I was a little girl, I was the only kid in the juniors who got a part, and afterwards we all got drunk — Where did all that bubbly come from, Richard?"

And you kissed me. And then you walked me home, and every girl in the school wanted to scratch out my eyes — wild Joan Lafferty who was only in second form, and my mother was waiting up, and when she saw the time she hit the roof, but not too much — she was married at seven-

teen, and you were a bank manager's son. Oh Dreamboat
Potter, what has happened to that skin smooth as jonquils
and the dreamboat eyes?

Ray Skerritt feels chilled, funny how you're always cold
in someone else's house. He moves over to the fire and
stands with his back to it. Angel Drimys, handing around
seaweed crackers, says "You and Joan manage time away
together, do you? I'd like Richard to take a few days off
this week during the school holidays." Ray says "Ah yes,
it's called flexi-time, isn't it? Us workers out at the mill
have flexi-time, too — start early and work late."

Angel Drimys doesn't laugh.

"And what's your line of business?" Ray jumps, turning
on Richard who is refilling Joan's glass.

God, I hope Ray's not going to get on one of his hob-
byhorses, Joan thinks, crinkling her forehead at him,
signalling this is a *holiday*.

"Have a drop more, Ray? I'm a public servant."

"You could have fooled me." Ray yanks off his tie.

"On Monday I rang your old department, Richard,"
Joan says quickly. "The one you were in when I bumped
into you in Melbourne. They redirected me."

"PM's? Yes, I've moved over to DAA now — Aboriginal
Affairs," he adds, as they look blank.

Angel Drimys, on her way out to the kitchen, says
"Richard's just back from a trip to the desert. Visiting
some of the communities."

"People who've gone back to their birthplace," Richard
explains. "Away from towns and whitefellers and booze."

"And you travel everywhere visiting them? How exciting!" Joan looks around the room and sees, upright as
spears, dried heads of evening primrose in an old-
fashioned bread crock. "I suppose you come back with all
sorts of things, shields and bark paintings and things."

"No. No, we don't do that," Richard says. "I did bring

this back, though." From the mantelpiece he takes a jar of red sand, its crystals glinting like sugar.

They pass the jar from one to another, shaking it, turning it so that the grains rush down the sides of the glass. Handing it back to Potter, Ray says "And are they happy to hear what Canberra's got to tell them?"

Richard laughs. "As much as anyone. Actually, our business is more listening than anything. Sitting down on the ground with the old men and listening. None of this belting questions at one another like rocks." He turns the jar of sand. "It takes time. Still . . . what's a few hours under a bloodwood compared with forty thousand years?"

Angel Drimys from the doorway says "Dinner's ready, everyone."

"She's been cooking venison," Emma adds. "Aren't you starving?"

"Last week I had roast *putjica*," Richard tells them, leading the way into the dining room where Angel at the table is lighting pale candles in shallow bowls of camellia. "Feral cat. They're all through the desert. Quite a delicacy, actually."

The House will divide

"Something I always feel after coming back from the desert," Richard says, looking around for somewhere to put the jar of sand and finally placing it on the table, "is this sense of dislocation. Joan, will you sit here? Trish —" He's got it all mapped out, Ray Skerritt thinks. Joan up there next to him and me way down here by his missus. When they are all seated Richard moves around the table filling the smaller of their glasses while Angel ladles out soup. Not much to chew on in *that*, Ray Skerritt decides, looking at the transparent liquid sprinkled with what seems to be dried grass. Oh good, there is sherry! thinks Joan, picking up her glass. She smiles at Richard: it's like the old days again, Chainsaw Potter at the centre and everyone gathered. She sips. Her mouth wrinkles against the sudden astringency. "It's hard to explain, the dislocation, I mean," Richard continues. "You're here and you're not here. Mind you, it only lasts a day or two. Then it's back to normal again."

"Yes, back to normal again," Angel echoes flatly, so that Joan stares. "And what do you all think of Canberra?" she says, catching Joan's glance. "Surprised? Disappointed?"

Yes! No! they reply, reminding themselves not to drink from the end of their soup spoons. It's beautiful. It's so clean. Those great wide streets. Blossom trees like weddings, offers Lurlene, giggling at her own daring. Great lot of building going on around the city, cranes everywhere. Great hands-off sculptures at the National Gallery, says Ray Skerritt, recalling Angel Drimys's instep. Great mountains, says Billy. You can see the snow from here.

"You should go skiing while you're here," Angel says. "Shouldn't they, Richard? Take a day off together to go skiing?"

Couldn't we, Dad? Billy's look pleads.

"Well . . ." Ray Skerritt laughs, thinking What would she know about the cost of taking five people for a day on the lifts?

"Oh but you must!" Angel insists. "Cross-country. Of course cross-country. It's so free. You go where you like. And economical. We love cross-country — don't we, Richard?"

"Ray and I met at the snow," Joan says dreamily. She was working at Falls Creek as a chambermaid, and Ray as a yardman, cleaning the dunnies and mopping up after the drunks, but she doesn't say that.

That the debate be adjourned

As Trish jumps up to help, Joan smiles: she's a good girl, Trish, easy, the easy one. On the kitchen table, amongst the preparation bowls and the vegetable peelings, Trish notices a small journal — poetry, she sees, glancing closer. On the cover is a familiar name. She picks it up.

"You like poetry?" Angel asks, turning from the stove where she is stirring red currant jelly into the gravy.

"Yes. No. I mean some, I like some. I saw Philip Jennaway's name on the cover —" She isn't explaining very well, and feels her face grow hot.

"Yes, I noticed there's something of his in that one. He's getting published everywhere these days. You like Jennaway?"

How funny it is to hear him called Jennaway, like Shakespeare or someone; it makes him seem out of reach, dead even. "Yes," she replies. Of course I like Phil! she wants to say. He's my cousin, he's family, of course I like him, it's only my sister —

"So do I," Angel is saying. "Jennaway's promising. One day he might even be good."

Good? Trish wants to laugh. Phil not good? Not a good person?

Angel is frowning. "I think . . . I think like a lot of people he's looking for answers instead of looking for questions. But that's the hard thing, isn't it, finding the questions. Anyone can come up with an answer. Of some sort. You can always dig out an answer from somewhere."

"Like wearing someone else's clothes," Trish says slowly. Angel glances at her, then goes on stirring. "Do you think it matters reading old stuff . . . Tennyson?" Trish ventures.

"Tennyson . . . *Yelled and shrieked between her daughters o'er a wild confederacy*. That always makes me smile, doesn't it you?" She lifts the stirring spoon, tastes, stirs again. "But there's lots more, isn't there? *Come down, O maid, from yonder mountain height*, and *murmuring of innumerable bees*. Can't you just hear those bees?"

"My sister doesn't like Tennyson."

"But do you, that's what matters."

Trish looks up in sudden gratitude.

"Richard says, he's finished carving the venison," says Emma at the doorway.

Angel takes the dinner plates from the warming oven. "Coming. Will you bring the gravy boat, Trish, please?"

The Honourable Member will draw her answer to a conclusion

"This red's a local." As Joan gazes in surprise at the minute amount Richard has poured in her glass, he adds "Try it, Joan, see if you like it. It's distinctive, this one. Fruity. Bit of a minx. Like it?" He fills her glass and moves around to Trish. "It's won a prize or two, actually. Canberra's well on the way to being Australia's cool climate wine capital, in my opinion."

"It's a lovely climate! People say Canberra's a freezing place but we've had nothing but sunshine every day." As the ruby red wine courses down to her toes, into the pit of her stomach, Joan smiles at Richard as though the good weather is something he has turned on for her.

"Just right for going to the snow," says Billy, looking at his father.

"Yes, it couldn't be better, Billy," Angel Drimys agrees, looking at her husband. "But the three-day forecast is for a change. For the snowfields, I mean. Richard! Rain!"

Richard sighs. "You know I can't get away right now, Angel."

Angel turns to Ray Skerritt with a brilliant smile. "That's what he said all last winter, Ray."

"Another trip coming up?" Ray asks Richard kindly. She's giving him a hard time. You wouldn't get her sort settling for a caravan park.

"Trip? No. Desk work. Most of my time is spent writing things in the office."

"Writing things?" Joan asks eagerly.

"Reports. Memos. Speeches for the Minister."

"No more plays, Chainsaw?"

"Plays? Plays?" He laughs. Joan winces. She thinks he is laughing at her. Dreamboat Potter, laughing at her.

"This dinner's wonderful, Angel!" she says, turning away. "Isn't it, Ray? I've never had venison before."

Billy leans across Angel Drimys to help himself to glazed chestnut. "They reckon there's deer up on Mount Hazelwood, Dad. You and me ought to get up there sometime with a gun."

"It's very . . . tasty," Trish offers shyly.

"Gamey," Ray Skerritt says, pleased at having thought of that, and glancing at Angel.

"Canberra," Angel says, staring past Ray. "You were saying about Canberra. Let me see, how do I see this city? As a place where so many of the necessities of life, time-consuming things I mean, like shopping, and travelling to the office, are so easy, so taken care of, so lacking in challenge compared with a really big city, that people here direct all their energies into *work!*"

A matter of public importance

"— this time, for instance," Richard Potter tells them, "Here we were sitting in a circle with men who saw their first whitefeller no more than maybe ten, even five years ago, and they were making a big effort to talk to us in English because they knew we couldn't speak a word of their language — " She's right. He does go on, Joan thinks. Not that it isn't interesting, Chainsaw Potter was always interesting, but it is a dinner party. "Listen Richard, they said, you whitefellers come over here all the way from the government and you tell us, Look here, you blackfellers can't start running cattle on the Myrrlumbing River, the Myrrlumbing River is a national park, that's the law, you blackfellers are living in a national park. We try to explain that national parks are state government business and we're federal not state government fellers. And they say, Richard, you go back and tell those government fellers, our people were here on this river long before national parks!"

"Cattle, eh?" says Ray. "I wouldn't like to see this — what is it? Myrrlumbing River turned into another dustbowl. Or another Ranger, either. How would they feel about that?"

As Richard starts to say something, Billy bursts out "I guess what they'd really like is for all us whities just to pack our gear and rack off!" He looks around the table . . . at his old man who might take him out shooting; at the fluttering candles like campfires in a garden; at the serving plates still half-full. Using his fork to spear another potato, he thinks *But rack off where* to?

"— go out with the seismic surveys," Richard Potter is saying.

"Your dinner's getting cold, Richard," Emma says, with a grin at her mother, so that Ray thinks *Poor bugger, it's a female conspiracy.*

"Myrrlumbing National Park." Angel swirls her glass slowly. "Not much left, is there, except the old names. Like some sort of sop to our consciences."

"Like Drimys," says Ray.

Angel laughs. "Drimys is not an indigenous word."

"But the shrub is."

"Australian? So am I."

"I'm glad to hear you say it!" Ray Skerritt exclaims, so that Trish jumps, wondering what lovely Mrs Potter has done to make her father sound angry. "I don't go for all this guilt business," Ray says. "I reckon that's just a sop too. Some bleeding heart's painkiller. Try a bit of guilt today, you'll feel on top again. Look, when trigger-happy bastards were running round down our way, I wasn't even born!"

Joan says quickly "We wouldn't sign that petition, would we, Ray? People in our street got up a petition a few years ago to have two Aboriginal families removed from council houses where they'd been resettled, because soon after they moved in, their cousins and friends turned up too, and they got drunk and wrecked up the houses and the neighbours complained but we wouldn't sign!"

Their eyes fix on the jar of sand in front of Richard Potter, its crystals the colour of dried blood.

Ring the bells! Lock the doors!

"No, no, no! Try to remember, girl." Glancing in Joan's direction, Ray Skerritt can scarcely keep the impatience out of his voice. "Like I told you — lean forward a bit. Bend your knees."

"I am remembering, Dad. I just need to practise," Trish says, going red as she wobbles again. Behind her, the navigation tower hums. She takes a lurching step. She's the only one left at the top of Mount Ginini. Billy and Lurlene are somewhere ahead. Along the snow-covered fire track her mother's red beanie is moving steadily.

"Lean forward —"

Alvie would just tell him to piss off. Trish takes a deep

breath. "You go on, Dad. I'll get the hang of it. Thanks."

Ray Skerritt sighs. "See you at the bottom, then."

He's pleased to find he hasn't forgotten. Skiing's like bicycling; or sex. Joan has almost reached the bend in the track. At Falls Creek she was always getting ahead. Something cold and slushy catches him on the neck. From behind a log crusted with old man's beard he hears Lurlene's shrill laugh. Those kids, he'll give them snowballs! Around the bend Joan is waiting for him. She rubs her cold nose against his cheek.

"Hello stranger."

"Listen," he says. "Joan. Next holiday we have, hang the expense, we're going to make damn' sure you and I have a room to ourselves, have a bit of fun, no more of this cooped up with a roomful of kids. Eh?"

Joan laughs. She claps her gloved hands. "Beat you to the bottom."

I think the ayes have it

Don't think about your feet, Trish tells herself. Don't look down. She shivers, alone in the shadow of the tower. A crow caws. Twigs spring back as their burdens of snow slide to the ground. *That coat you wear, Trish.* It isn't mine. It doesn't belong — That won't do. She starts again. By the way, Trish, that's a lovely coat. That coat suits you. The voice has become Angel Drimys's. Trish breathes deeply. Isn't it! Doesn't it!

Now, says Trish, lifting her face to the cold air. She pushes one foot, then the other forward in long, smooth, gliding steps. She is moving. *The shallop flitteth silken-sailed* she sings as she progresses steadily over the track, past a straggly nest of crows, past the green-boughed, twisted gums where clumps of snow are lustrous with sunlight.